Curtis Creed

and the
Lore of the Ocean

By
Rebecca Fraser

To Thea

Wishing you a very
Happy Birthday

With very best wishes

Rebecca x

Curtis Creed and the Lore of the Ocean

All Rights Reserved

ISBN-13: 978-1-925759-03-7

Copyright ©2018 Rebecca Fraser

V1.0

Printed in Palatino Linotype and Gaudy Old Style.

IFWG Publishing Australia

www.ifwgaustralia.com

Acknowledgements

No book comes into the world without support, encouragement, and opportunity. To this end, I would like to offer my sincere thanks to the following people:

Gerry Huntman and IFWG Publishing Australia for taking Curtis Creed's story on board (see what I did there?), Dr Jane Messer of Macquarie University for inspiring me to continually challenge myself, Dr Elizabeth Claire Alberts (environmental journalist, and one of the best friends our planet could have) for her thoughtful feedback and advice.
And lastly, to my dear family, who are, and always have been, my constant cheer squad and steadfast supporters of my creative endeavours. And to Steve, my anchor. Thank you. Thank you so much.

For Thomas, with an ocean of love

But more wonderful than the lore of old men

and the lore of books

is the secret lore of ocean.

- H P Lovecraft

CHAPTER 1

Curtis Creed stood at the water's edge. *Come back to me,* the ocean sighed. *Come back to me.* But he couldn't. Not today. Not ever.

He squinted against the afternoon sun and focused on the line-up of surfers gathered out past the second break. Even though they were far offshore, Curtis' trained eye was able to pick out their various styles and techniques—weight transfers, body positions, timing. It was second nature. If you weren't in the surf yourself then you were watching other surfers; scrutinising their moves, checking out technique.

He'd stood at the shoreline for so long his feet had become anchored, buried ankle-deep in the sand with the ebb and pull of the tide. Out among the breakers, a surfer powered down the face of a beautifully formed wave before disappearing into the pipeline. *Remember that feeling?* the ocean breathed. *Remember?* Of course he remembered, but he couldn't return to the surf. He just couldn't.

Instead the school holidays dragged along, lonesome days spent wandering the shoreline of Midnight Cove or sitting high up on The Bluff, watching others chase waves. Sometimes, when the surf was really pumping, his sense of loss and failure was so suffocating it was easier to avoid the beach altogether.

Thwack. A wad of wet sand hit Curtis hard in the back, right between his shoulders. His buried feet caused him to lose balance and he pitched forward. He flung his arms out to steady himself too late and landed in the water on all fours.

"Whatcha doing, Shark Crumb? Looking out for sharks?" The hated nickname. Loud guffaws. It was Dylan and his moronic mates. Why couldn't his brother just leave him alone?

"Yeah, Shark Crumb. Seen any sharks lately?"

"Better get out of the water, Shark Crumb. They'll smell your fear."

Curtis stood up. His board shorts and the front of his singlet were soaked. He turned to face his tormentors. Dylan was flanked by Blake and Jordo, two of his mates from high school. They were fresh from the surf with wetsuits pulled down around their waists. Water dripped from their hair and trickled down their torsos. The boys had pressed their surfboards into the wet sand, where they stood upright like silent sentinels.

Then Curtis noticed Dylan was using their father's surfboard and anger boiled inside him like lava in a volcano. The thruster stood between Blake and Jordo's boards, a falcon between two pigeons. It was handcrafted for speed and could cut down the face of a wave like no other. Dimples of wax glinted from its surface, wax that remained from another time, applied in dawn's first light by their father's hand. The image sliced Curtis' heart as cleanly as the board's fin cut through water.

"Why have you got Dad's board?" He was screaming now. He couldn't help it. Didn't care.

"What's it to you? You never use it." Dylan folded his arms across his chest.

"That's not the point." Curtis took a step closer to Dylan. "Dad left it to me. To *me*." His voice was shaking now. Blake and Jordo circled like a pair of seagulls, cawing out the familiar taunt *Shark Crumb*, but Curtis barely heard them.

A tendon in Dylan's neck began to pulse. He shaped up to Curtis so closely he could see the peppering of blackheads across Dylan's nose. "Dad never would've left it to you if he knew you were going to turn into such a pussy."

Before he'd even thought about what he was doing, Curtis punched Dylan in the face as hard as he could. The swing harnessed every ounce of his rage and the punch landed with a clap. Dylan fell backwards. His eyes widened with surprise then quickly clouded with danger. A droplet of blood fell from his nose and made a coin-sized stain on the wet sand.

It was time to go. Curtis turned and pelted off down the beach. Behind him he could hear Blake and Jordo give chase, but he knew he could outrun them. The stupid nickname rang out behind him, but as the distance grew the voices became fainter until they were eventually torn away by the ocean breeze.

He ran without looking back. His breath hitched in his chest. A ball of embers burned the back of his throat, but still he ran. Tears stung his eyes, but he also felt a thrill of exhilaration. He'd hit Dylan before, of course, and received his fair share back. Heck, they were brothers. They'd grown up with horse bites, birthday punches, Chinese burns, and the dreaded typewriter. But he'd never all out hauled off and decked him. It had felt good, but the brief rush of exhilaration was quickly replaced by terror at the thought of what awaited him when he returned home. Especially as he'd managed to floor Dylan in front of his mates. His brother would no doubt have all kinds of retribution in store.

He decided to delay for as long as he could. As he rounded the southernmost end of Midnight Cove he slowed to a jog. Here the long stretch of beach gave way to a rocky shoreline heavily strewn with ancient lava boulders and rock pools. The rock shelf—a labyrinth of stones and shallows— skirted the great cliffs that rose to form Midnight Bluff, the town's highest point.

The ocean's teeth had gnashed the cliffs for thousands of years carving an alien landscape of rock face and rivulets. The rock pools closest to the sandy beach made safe watery playgrounds for children to explore with buckets and spades. Further round the headland, however, access was difficult and discouraged. The gentle waves that undulated through the bay had nowhere to go when they met land here, and they boomed and crashed over the rocks. The boulders were larger and denser, filled with ankle-breaking crevices and rock pools that were deceptively deeper than their beach-hugging counterparts. They filled and drained with the tide's highs and lows.

Curtis knew Dylan wouldn't follow him here. It wasn't just the difficulty of access that would stop him, there were too many memories.

Curtis ignored his aching fist as he jumped gazelle-like from boulder to boulder. The ocean's salt-tinged air whipped and whistled and he ventured deeper into the network of rock pools until the beach was completely out of sight.

CHAPTER 2

The boulders were warm from the afternoon sun. They felt comforting beneath Curtis' bare feet. He scrambled over them, wading through shallow pools formed by centuries of water forging their designs into the rocky shelf.

He avoided stepping into the larger pools where the bottom depths were obscured by russet-coloured seaweeds that swayed gently on their anchors. He was conscious of unseen threats: cone shells, blue-ringed octopi, stone fish, and other venomous creatures. Crabs skittered at his tread, and scores of miniature silver fish darted as one as his shadow fell across their waters.

The further Curtis travelled, the calmer he began to feel. His heart still pounded from the altercation with Dylan, but the ocean's rhythm was soothing, and he knew where he was headed. He picked his way around another half dozen rock pools and there was the boulder. It had always been recognisable with its distinctive trapezoid shape. It was even more so now, although the bouquet of plastic flowers fastened to it always seemed garish and out of place. As Curtis scrambled up the boulder's flat, grey side he saw the impossible blues and oranges of the flowers' petals had faded further since he was last here. He wanted to tell Mum but knew she'd be furious with him for venturing here in the first place. *What were you thinking Curtis?* she would say. *It's far too dangerous. You know it only takes one wave to come over the rocks and then—* He pictured her face; her eyes would flame with anger, then it would crumple and sag as the tears came. He didn't want to make her cry. She still cried a lot. Sometimes he heard her muffled sobs from places she thought he and Dylan wouldn't hear. Hidden beneath the shower's stream of water, or late at night behind the closed door of her bedroom.

Instead he took the bouquet from the metal cylinder that housed it and plucked the petals that had faded the most. He manipulated the remainders on their green plastic stem, twisting them to cover the empty spaces, and replaced the bouquet. The cylinder was attached to the rock with metal screws, and Curtis noticed they were starting to rust. Fading and rusting. Sometimes he worried this would happen to his memories of his father.

He couldn't talk about it with Dylan, of course. He'd changed so much since Dad had gone. Dylan never came out here, never talked about what happened. It was almost like his brother—the old Dylan, the one who would never let his friends call him names, let alone do it himself—had died with his father.

"I'm not a pussy, Dad," Curtis said. The ocean roared her response, and sent a wall of whitewash over the boulders. He watched the water surge into furrows and gutters, filling the rock pools. The wind snatched the plucked petals from his hand before he could save them, and played with them before depositing them in the pool below. There they danced and swirled before they were sucked out to sea with the retreating water. Curtis wondered if they would find his father.

The ocean roared again, but this time he heard something else. A high-pitched noise, faint but distinct. Curtis cocked his head and listened. There it was again. Louder this time. And again—a wailing call of distress on the ocean breeze. He stood up and looked in the direction of the noise. It was coming from the south. Curtis knew instinctively that it was a cry of pain—he also knew that it didn't sound human.

He jumped down from the trapezoid rock—*Dad's rock*—and followed the cries, scrambling as fast as he dared over the slippery, barnacle-crusted rocks. It wasn't long until he came to a large pool, sheltered from the ocean by a curved rock ledge.

There, amid the kelp and the sea grass, was the source of the noise. At first Curtis' eyes simply refused to believe what they were seeing. Someone, or *something*, thrashed in the pool below. It looked like a girl, but something wasn't right. He blinked and processed. Yes, it was shaped like a girl—two arms, two legs, head where it should be—but it was all wrong.

The girl-thing's mouth opened—*teeth, sharp pointed teeth*—and gave voice to another great wail of pain. The sound reminded him of when old Mrs Webster's miniature poodle had been hit by a car. He'd found the little dog's misshapen, bloodied body on the curb side outside their house, and when he ran his hand gently along its matted fur to comfort it, it had howled its distress across the neighbourhood. The sound had dried the spit in his mouth.

He crouched lower in an effort to remain unseen and peered into the water to see if he could determine what was ailing the stranger. His long hair flopped across his face and he brushed it from his eyes. The girl-creature flailed again, exposing a slender leg—a fin? Was that a fin on her leg?—and Curtis saw in an instant what the trouble was. He knew he could help and with her next cry of pain, he sprang into action.

CHAPTER 3

Curtis scrambled crablike down the rocky embankment and landed in the rock pool with a splash. He was submerged to his knees. Slimy tendrils of seaweed grabbed at his ankles as he waded towards the girl. *No, not a girl*, his mind rejected. *Not a human girl anyway. She was some sort of...creature.* She was still now. His entrance had caused whatever she was to stop thrashing. Her head—*what was that on her head?*—turned towards him and a pair of the strangest eyes he had ever seen regarded him with wary suspicion. They were a brilliant shade of green with dark vertical pupils more suited to a cat—long, thin and almond-shaped.

Curtis' heart thundered against his ribcage, but it was too late to turn back now, he was only metres from her. He held up his hands to show he meant no harm and edged towards her. "It's okay. I can help. I...um...I come in peace." He knew that last bit sounded ridiculous, but couldn't think what else to say. The creature's pupils dilated and she peeled back her lips. He caught another glimpse of her mouth tightly filled with tiny, pointed teeth, and gulped.

"Easy, easy." Curtis took a slow step forward. He was so close now he could see what puzzled him about the creature's head. It was covered in coral. It grew in a swirling, intricate pattern that reminded him of the detail on his mother's filigree pendant. The coral encased the creature's head and ran down the bridge of her nose and length of her neck. It clad her head like a medieval knight's helmet. The face it framed,

9

while distorted with pain and fear, had fine, sculpted features. Where the coral stopped at the base of her head, Curtis noticed what looked like a blowhole at her nape. It flapped rapidly, opening and closing, spraying a fine mist across her back and shoulders.

Curtis kept his hands up as he lowered into a squat. "It's okay. I know I can help you. If you'll let me..." He trailed off and slowly, ever so slowly, eased himself into the water. Emerald eyes locked on his. Her teeth bared. Curtis reached out and tentatively put a hand on her side. Her skin felt leathery and cold. It rippled at his touch, but she allowed him to gently run his hand down her leg. Curtis' heart beat wildly as he worked his way down to where the trouble was. He expected sharp teeth to sink into him at any moment, but the creature only blazed at him with her strange eyes.

"Okay, I'm going to duck under the water now. It's going to hurt a bit, but I reckon I can get it done pretty quickly, okay?" Silence from the creature. "Um, okay then, so here I go." Curtis took a deep breath and put his head under the water. The salt stung his eyes, and he blinked them rapidly to clear his vision. A length of fishing line had wrapped around the creature's ankle and embedded itself deep into her flesh. As Curtis worked, quickly unwinding the tangle of line, he marvelled at her form. Rather than fishlike scales, her skin was smooth like an eel. Her body was human in form, but built for the ocean. Her calves were adorned with graceful fins of the lightest salmon colour; her feet appeared normal but a fine membrane of webbing connected her toes. Dappled sun filtering through the water gave her skin a pearlescent tinge. What was this strange creature, he wondered? She had the body of a human girl, yet seemed equipped with amphibious features. It just wasn't possible.

When Curtis had unwound the last of the fishing line, he saw a hook was also involved. Exhaling the last of his breath, he tugged sharply. As the hook came free, a burst of violet-coloured blood erupted from the wound.

Curtis emerged from the water and held the line and hook

10

aloft triumphantly. "Got it," he cried. "Fishing line, see? Must've been left behind by a rock fisherman." Somewhere in the distance of his mind strode an image of his father, rod in hand, but he wasn't going to think of that now.

The creature had pulled herself into a sitting position. She ignored Curtis and moved her hands along the walls of the rock pool, searching for something among the limpets and barnacles. At last she found what she sought and pulled it free. Curtis noticed the same webbing that was between her toes also connected her long, graceful fingers. Delicate fins decked her outer arms from wrist to elbow.

It was an anemone she held. Its tentacles retracted from the sunlight as she lifted it from the water. She bought the jelly-like blob to her mouth and bit into it with her sharp teeth. The anemone oozed, and she quickly wiped the gelatinous substance onto the cut on her ankle. The blood stemmed immediately. She turned to Curtis and said something unintelligible. Her voice sounded like his grandmother's wind chimes when the steel tubes clanged together.

"Sorry?" Curtis shook his head. "I don't understand."

The creature tried again. This time she spoke English.

"They won't catch my scent now." Her words sounded watery and melodic.

"Sharks?"

The creature put her head to one side in a silent question.

"Sharks," Curtis repeated, "they can smell blood."

"Sharks are harmless. They do not concern me."

Curtis scratched his head for a moment. "Are you a mermaid?"

"Mermaids are the fancy of humans."

"Are you a… a…" Curtis searched his mind for the folklore he'd learned last year at school. "A Siren?"

"No. I am Navaya."

"What's a Navaya?"

"I am Navaya, daughter and protector of Araxie."

"Oh. I am Curtis. Um…son of Lori and Robert."

"Thank you, Curtis, for your help. Your good deed will be

retold and remembered by the Arax."

"The Arax? What are the Arax? And what did you mean when you said they won't catch your scent? Who were you talking about?"

"Glynts," Navaya said. The word dropped from her mouth, dark and guttural. Even though the afternoon sun was still hot on his back, Curtis felt a trickle of ice run down his spine.

"What are Glynts?" Even as he asked the question, he felt he didn't want to know.

"Abominations," Navaya spat. "Vipers from the deepest oceans. Enemy of Araxie. Enemy to your human race too."

"What do you mean? I've never heard of a Glynt, or an Arax, or anything before today." He stopped to consider. "I don't think anyone else has either."

"Of course you haven't. Arax and Glynt are rarely seen by human eyes. And those that have seen a Glynt have not lived to talk of it. It doesn't matter. I doubt you'll see either again in your lifetime." As Navaya spoke, she rose from the water to scan the ocean beyond the curved rock ledge. "The passage looks clear now." Out of the water, the pearlescent sheen of her skin was more pronounced. It shimmered in the sun like the inside of an abalone shell. Her body was sheathed in a garment made from what appeared to be a type of seaweed he knew as Neptune's Necklace. Strings of the olive-brown beads had been woven together to form a tunic that covered her torso to thigh. She lowered herself back into the rock pool.

"Did they catch your scent? Is that how you ended up here?"

"No. I wasn't bleeding when they attacked. I must go now. I've said too much," Navaya said.

"You were attacked? By Glynts? Why?" Curtis leaned forward, fascinated and fearful at the same time. "Were they going to eat you?"

"A Glynt could never hope to digest an Arax." Navaya's face grew scornful. "They want to steal this." She stroked the skin around her neck. Her eyes grew round as her fingers searched frantically. "The Moami. It's gone." She began a frenzied search of the rock pool, moving around the shallows on her belly, her streamlined body making rapid turns at each end.

Eventually she raised her head. Water streamed from her coral headpiece. "It's not here. I must have lost it when I was being chased." Navaya's blowhole opened and closed wildly and Curtis now saw it was framed by a black pattern, not unlike the tribal tattoos some older surfers had inked on their backs or biceps.

"Is it important?" Curtis ventured, although he could tell by Navaya's anxious search that it was.

"The Moami is a key. The Glynts have wanted it since the first cycle of the moon held sway over the first ocean. But there I go spouting off again. The others are always saying I talk too much."

"But why do they want it?" Curtis pinched himself hard to make sure he wasn't dreaming, or had slipped and hit his head on a rock and Navaya was a hallucination.

"They want what we have."

"What's that?" His arm hurt from the pinch.

"I don't have time to explain. I've already broken Araxie law by letting you see me, but as a protector of Arax, I need your help. The Glynts *must not* find the Moami. If they do, the Arax—humans too—will be in great danger. I need you to help me search. Will you help me find the Moami, Curtis, son of Lori and Robert?" Navaya's green eyes held his blue ones.

"But what can *I* do to help?" Curtis said. "I don't know anything about Araxie laws, or keys, or moon cycles or Glynts." *Besides, I don't even go in the water anymore.* His troubles with Dylan seemed a very long way away.

"Check the shore. The Moami may have washed up on the beach. I cannot venture where I risk being seen."

"But how will I know what it looks like?"

"Here, I will draw it for you." Navaya leapt from the rock pool. The movement was graceful and sleek. She found a patch of damp sand between two boulders, knelt down and traced an image with her finger. The webbing between her fingers flexed and contracted with the movement, and the fins on her arms and legs fluttered in the afternoon breeze like the gossamer wings of a butterfly. Her coral-clad head bowed in concentration.

Curtis studied her as she worked. He took in every detail of her impossible body so he could recall it later and convince himself again he hadn't been dreaming.

"Here, the Moami looks like this." She tapped the image with her index finger. Curtis squatted next to her. She had drawn what appeared to be a necklace holding a circular pendant. The pendant bore the same markings as those that ringed her blowhole: angular lines softened by swirling loops creating a pattern as deep as the ocean itself.

"It's an amulet," Curtis said.

"Not an amulet. The Moami is a key." She spoke slowly, as if explaining to a small child. "It looks like an amulet, yes. The cord that holds it is whale leather, and the Moami itself is carved from an underwater metal. Your kind would know it as a form of cobalt."

"Cobalt is blue, right?" Curtis pushed hair from his eyes to better study the image. The pattern was so detailed, he wished he had a camera to photograph it. "I can go search the shore right now. The stretch that runs from one end of the bay to the other anyway. I'll come right back."

"Not today. The tide is rising and these pools will soon be submerged. Besides, I must search the ocean floor. I covered a great distance fleeing the Glynts. I know the Moami was still intact when I passed the third current, so it must have been lost somewhere beyond." Navaya looked towards the sun. It had made its lazy arc across the sky and now hovered low against the horizon. "Check the shore now while the tide is high, and again in the morning when it is low. These are the times when the ocean chooses to reveal her bounty. See where the sun is now? I will meet you back here when it's in the same position tomorrow."

"Okay, I hope you find it. And if you don't, then I hope I do."

"Thank you, Curtis. As I said, your good deeds will be retold and remembered by the Arax. But you must tell no one. Not about me, and not of the Moami. Can I trust you?" Her voice had taken on a dangerous edge, and Curtis wondered what would happen if he said no. Would rows of pointed teeth sink into his throat and tear at his flesh? Would her long, strong fingers clamp around his throat? Her eyes told a different story though, and he sensed that Navaya, whatever she was, was a creature he could trust.

Besides, who would he possibly tell? Certainly not Dylan. His mother would want to take him straight back to Dr Mackenzie, and Tyler and Lachlan, his two best mates, were both away for the school holidays.

"You can trust me, Navaya." Curtis said. And he realised he meant it.

"May the lore of the ocean aid you in your search." Navaya sprang lithely from boulder to boulder until she faced the ocean. Waves crested and coursed about the rocks, shooting foam high into the air as they broke. "And if you do find it, watch out for Glynts," she shouted, before plunging into the deep blue in a perfectly timed surge of backwash.

CHAPTER 4

Curtis hit the shoreline of Midnight Cove at a run. He'd made the journey back through the rock pools and lava boulders on autopilot as he scrambled to recall every detail of Navaya, what she had said, and what the Moami looked like.

Back in familiar territory the craziness of what just happened crashed over him like a wave. *Talking sea creatures don't exist,* his mind clamoured. *Don't they? Why not? Just because you've never seen one before, doesn't mean they're not real,* another part of his mind argued.

He ran his hand over his left forearm. The purplish bruise blooming under his skin from his pinch was real. So was the salt-white tightness of seawater drying on his skin from his soaking in the rock pool.

The wet, granular sand sank beneath his feet as he combed the shore for any sign of the amulet. *Key,* he corrected himself. *Not an amulet, a key. A key to what?* He worked his way methodically along the tide line, stopping to lift up clumps of streaky kelp and other debris that had been deposited along the beach.

There was no sign of Dylan and his cronies now, and the beach was empty except for a few lone beachcombers and joggers. He kept his eyes to the sand as they passed him, returning their greetings without looking up. His heart lurched when he spotted a hint of blue up ahead. He hurried towards it but it was only a blue bottle, its azure sail poking up deceptively from the sand. Curtis exhaled the breath he'd been holding and nudged the jellyfish with his toe. There was no sign of the Moami.

He continued his search until he reached the other end of Midnight Cove, then turned back again, eyes scanning the shore for anything he may have missed. There was just the usual detritus: broken shells, pebbles, tangles of seaweed, and the odd cuttlebone.

He thought of Navaya as he walked. Imagined her searching the ocean floor, her supple body cutting through the water. He looked out to sea and for a moment fancied he could see a blowhole spouting, but it was just whitecaps dancing in the last rays of the afternoon sun.

He was nearly at the exit that would lead him back to the esplanade, and decided he would start the search again at first light tomorrow. The tide may reveal its secrets overnight and he needed to be the first person to find them.

Up ahead a girl swept the sand back and forth with a metal detector. Curtis had seen people do this before of course, but it was normally old men stooping along in their socks and sandals. As he got closer, he saw the girl was about his age. She had long, cinnamon-coloured hair, and the palest skin he had ever seen. It was the colour of milk. Freckles the same colour as her hair were sprinkled liberally across her body and face, and she wore a sunhat with a brim so wide it seemed to throw out as much shade as his mother's striped beach umbrella.

Swish-swish. Back and forth went the metal detector. Every now and then the girl would stop and plunge into the sand with a little scoop, then shake it like a sieve to examine its contents.

A little thrill ran through him at what she may have discovered. He went up to her. "Hi there," he greeted. "Found anything exciting?"

The girl peered at him from under the brim of her hat with serious grey eyes. "If by exciting you mean a bunch of ring pulls, bottle tops, and a ten cent piece, I guess so."

"Oh well, better luck next time," Curtis said. He turned and walked away. He'd put a fair bit of distance between them when the idea struck him.

"Hey," he called, and jogged back. "I don't suppose that thing can detect cobalt, can it?" he asked.

"Um, I don't know," the girl said. "I only just got it. It was a Christmas present. Don't think so. Why? Have you lost something with cobalt in it?"

Oh, no reason…just curious. Okay, gotta run. See ya." He turned and sped towards the dunes before she could answer. He thought he heard the girl call out after him, but by this time he'd hit the track that led off the beach and didn't look back.

Sand gave way to dirt, and the dunes gave way to grassy hillocks, thick with vegetation. Curtis wove between clusters of crooked pandanus trees until the track pushed him out onto the foreshore and the suburban landscape of Midnight Cove.

He turned towards home. In spite of the mood Dylan would be in, he felt more alive than he had in months. Tomorrow he would see Navaya again. He would find the Moami and return it to her if he could, and he'd ask all the questions that buzzed across his mind like a swarm of bees. What exactly were Glynts and Arax? Why had no one seen one before? Were there others like her? And what had she meant about humans being under threat? Was there really danger?

The school holidays were shaping up to be not so boring after all. His neighbourhood was like the rest of Midnight Cove—green expanses of lawn punctuated with hibiscus bushes, jacaranda, and the occasional mango tree. Red brick houses rubbed shoulders with character-filled Queenslanders sitting proudly on their wooden stumps. He passed the normal-looking houses in their normal-looking streets, his mind reeling with the knowledge that the normal people of Midnight Cove didn't know what he knew. He had a secret.

CHAPTER 5

The fly wire door of the Creed's faded weatherboard home gave its usual protesting creak. "Hey Mum, I'm home." Curtis made his way to the kitchen and pulled open the fridge door. He scanned its contents for anything new before pulling out a carton of orange juice. He chugged it straight from the carton, flinching in anticipation of his mum's scolding. He could never see the point in dirtying a glass, especially when it was he who had to wash them.

But Mum wasn't there. As he closed the fridge he noticed a slip of paper held in place by a plastic magnet in the shape of a pineapple. It was a note in her looping handwriting. *Working a double shift tonight. Sorry, boys. Won't be home until late. Shepherd's pie in the oven. See you in the morning. Mum xx*

His mum worked at the old people's home on the western side of Midnight Cove. She wore a navy blue uniform with white soft-soled shoes. Curtis reckoned she smelled funny whenever she came home from working there. It must be old person smell, he figured. Or the food. He'd seen it once when Mum had asked him and Dylan to help out on an Open Day. He'd pushed a trolley of steaming bowls where weird grey lumps floated alongside peas and carrots in a gloopy stew. Mum worked a lot of double shifts since Dad had gone.

Curtis opened the oven door to inspect the shepherd's pie.

"I should shove your head right into that oven."

He leapt up. Dylan sprawled across the kitchen bench. The left side of his face looked swollen, and a hint of purple-black shadow had started to blemish the skin around his eye.

"Get stuffed, Dylan," Curtis shot back. "You shouldn't have been using Dad's board."

Dylan made a lunge for him across the bench. Curtis side-stepped it neatly. When Dylan grabbed at him in a fresh attack, Curtis noticed something in his hand. Something that flashed blue.

"What's that you've got?" Curtis sprang back out of Dylan's reach.

"Something I found on the beach." He held up his find. A circular pendant swung on a length of cord. Curtis gaped. It was a disc of lustrous silver-grey metal carved in an intricate pattern. Flecks of brightest blue caught the light as it swung back and forth like a pendulum.

The Moami. Dylan had the Moami.

"What d'ya reckon, Shark Crumb?" Dylan said, his fight forgotten as he studied the pendant. "I reckon that blue stuff is topaz, or some other precious gem. Sapphire maybe."

"Cobalt." Curtis' voice was air escaping from a balloon.

"Huh?"

"Nothing." *Dylan has the Moami. Dylan has the Moami,* his mind jabbered. "Where did you find it?" he asked, trying not to let his face or voice betray anything other than a passing interest.

"On the beach where you managed to throw your lucky punch. It was right on the shoreline where you were standing. Surprised you didn't trip over it when you ran away like the pussy you are."

Curtis ignored his jibe. "Let me see." He stretched out his hand. As soon as Dylan handed it over he was going to run faster than a dingo from a bushfire.

"Fat chance. I'm going to give it to Kiara. She's gonna love it." Dylan coiled up the Moami and stuffed it into his pocket.

"But you can't do that," Curtis protested. "It's not yours."

"So what," Dylan said. "Finders keepers. It's the law of the beach."

"That's bull, Dylan, you just made that up." He wanted to

fly across the kitchen counter and tackle Dylan. He would wrestle him to the ground and pin his arms behind his back. He'd reach into his pocket and —

"Whatever, Shark Crumb. It's not like you know whose it is. What do you even care anyway? I'm gonna ring Kiara. See ya, wouldn't wanna be ya." Dylan sauntered into the lounge room and flopped onto the couch with his mobile phone.

Curtis felt like he'd been axed by a dumper and was fighting the whitewash. How was he going to get his hands on the Moami now? Kiara was Dylan's girlfriend. They'd become an item during the last year and as far as Curtis could tell their relationship consisted mostly of long talks about nothing over the phone, endless text messages, milkshakes at the kiosk, and holding hands across the water as they sat side-by-side on their boards while they waited for the next set to roll in.

If Curtis had a girlfriend like Kiara, he would do more exciting things than that. She was tall and tanned with a mane of exotic hair, treacle-flecked on the tips where the sun had bleached it. When she laughed a dimple bounced in her left cheek. She could carve it up better than most guys her age and she never called him Shark Crumb. Whenever she smiled at him his mouth filled with cotton wool and he could barely speak.

"I've got something for you, babe. You're going to love it." Dylan's voice drifted from the lounge room. "Yeah, that's right, a present. Come over in the morning, I'll give it to you before I hit the surf."

Curtis went to his room. He shut the door and lay on his bed. What was he going to do now? What would he say to Navaya if he couldn't get the Moami back? He couldn't tell Dylan about her. He'd promised.

His eyes drifted about his room. Posters of his heroes adorned the walls. Mick Fanning, Kelly Slater, Taj Burrow, Occy, Stephanie Gilmour, Joel Parkinson, Owen Wright. They were captured for eternity in technicoloured glory — surfing epic barrels, tearing up the waves in their signature styles.

His eyes travelled to his trophy shelves. They were filled

with evidence of his own triumphs: medals and ribbons on display amid an assortment of trophies and cups, all engraved with his name. *Curtis Creed, Age Champion. First Place—Grommet Surf Titles. Best in Break—Curtis Creed. State Age Champion—Curtis Creed.*

He rolled over and looked at the wall. Dylan's words to Kiara came back to him. *"Come over in the morning, I'll give it to you before I hit the surf."* It wasn't that long ago that he'd hit the surf every morning too.

He pushed the thought to the chamber at the back of his mind where shadows and memories lurked, then slammed the door. He concentrated on the day's events instead, recalling every aspect of his meeting with Navaya. Freeing her from the fishing line, her talk of the Arax and how she was sworn to protect Araxie. And of course, Glynts. He wished he'd asked more about them. He wondered again what she'd meant when she said they were dangerous to humans as well. They filled him with an unnamed horror, and when he finally slept that night his dreams were of fearsome serpents that seethed and writhed in the blue-black depths of the ocean.

CHAPTER 6

Sunlight probed his bedroom with golden fingers, accompanied by the perfumed scent of frangipani drifting through his open window. Curtis blinked and yawned. His head felt muzzy from too much sleep.

He could hear voices in the kitchen. Every now and then the muted conversation was interrupted by a tinkle of laughter. *Kiara*. Kiara was here.

He rolled out of bed and hunted for a clean t-shirt, then raked his fingers through his hair like a comb knowing it would do little to detangle his shoulder length locks. He went to the bathroom, peed, and then turned on the cold tap to splash water onto his face. As he groped for a towel, he wondered if Dylan had presented Kiara with the Moami yet.

"Oh, Dylan. I *love* it." Kiara's voice floated down the hallway answering Curtis' question. He groaned, put the towel down, and padded towards the kitchen. The floorboards felt cold beneath his bare feet, matching the chill he felt at her words. Getting the Moami back from Dylan was challenge enough, how was he going to get it now Kiara had it? What would Navaya say? Or do?

"Curtis, look what Dylan gave me," Kiara burst as he entered the room. The Moami was around her neck. She lifted the cord so he could better see. On the other side of the kitchen table Dylan smugly chewed a piece of toast.

Curtis came forward on wooden legs. The Moami swung back and forth. It caught the rays of the morning sun and threw them prism-like across the room. Blue shadows danced across the ceiling and Kiara's face.

"Oh, wow, Kiara…that's really cool." He reached out his hand and she let the Moami drop into his palm. It was the first time he'd seen it up close, and he marvelled at the intricacy of the carving, the brilliance of the blue from the cobalt flecks ingrained throughout. He closed his fingers around the disc and for a moment something pulsed through his body like electricity. It surged through his cells like a dart of adrenalin.

"Isn't it exquisite?" Her fingers brushed his and the moment was gone.

"I've never seen anything like it," Curtis said truthfully. *Or felt anything like it. What was that all about? Had Kiara felt it too? She didn't act like she had.* He looked pointedly at Dylan, "Wherever did you get it?"

Dylan glared at him across the table. "I have my sources," he replied.

"Because, you know, if you *found* something like that, you'd have to try and find the owner. You couldn't just give it away."

"Thanks for your input, Shark Crumb. No need to trouble your tiny mind." Dylan emphasized this by drawing his finger slowly and deliberately across his throat. Kiara was too engrossed in examining her gift to notice the exchange.

Curtis boiled with embarrassment. He hated the nickname at the best of times, but even more so when Dylan used it around Kiara. He crossed to the fridge and poured himself a glass of milk. If he could just get Dylan out of the room, he might have a chance to get his hands on the Moami. His mind ticked with possible solutions. One was definitely worth a try.

"Conditions are gonna be awesome this morning," he said. "Heaps of barrel opps. I wouldn't leave it too late though…" He trailed off as if he'd been talking to himself, but it worked.

Dylan checked the old clock that hung on the kitchen wall, and pushed his chair back. "Sorry, babe, I gotta run. Surf's gonna be pumping."

"That's okay. I've got to go to work anyway." Kiara was already dressed in her Curlz uniform. Curlz was one of Midnight Cove's surf stores. Kiara worked weekends and holiday shifts, selling surf apparel and accessories to locals and tourists.

"I'll just grab my stuff." Dylan threw a dangerous look in Curtis' direction before he left the room.

Curtis took his milk to the table. Being so close to Kiara made him feel light headed. The floral scent of her freshly-washed hair, the tan lines from her bikini just visible beneath the crisp white of her Curlz shirt, the way her eyes shone as she examined the Moami.

"Would it be okay if I had a proper look, Kiara?"

She smiled at him and a flock of tiny birds took wing across his stomach. "Of course. Here." Kiara took the Moami from around her neck and handed it across the table. "Your brother sure can be a sweetheart when he wants to be."

He had it. The Moami was in his hand. The vibration he'd felt earlier throbbed through his body like a heartbeat. *Run, Curtis,* it seemed to say. *Run.* He knew this was his chance. Slowly, very slowly, he got up. Then slowly, very slowly, he stepped away from the table. All the while he held the Moami up and made admiring noises so Kiara wouldn't get suspicious. She smiled at him again and the flock of birds wheeled and swooped. He felt sick that it was Kiara he had to disappoint. *Damn you, Dylan. Why did it have to be Dylan who'd found it?*

He was almost to the other side of the kitchen now. Soon, he would turn and bolt. He would run even faster than he did yesterday when Jordo and Blake were chasing him, and he wouldn't stop until he was deep into the Bluff's rocky landscape safely past Dad's memorial rock. Then he would wait by the rock pool for Navaya.

Closer now, so close. Just one final step and he would be out of the room. He took a deep breath and stepped backwards—

—straight into Dylan.

Dylan leaned forward and plucked the Moami neatly out of Curtis' fingers. As it left his grasp, a cold stone dropped into the pit of his stomach. *No. He had been so close.*

"What the hell's gotten into you?" Dylan hissed in his ear.

He crossed to Kiara and replaced the length of whale hide around her neck. The Moami settled between the gentle swell of her chest, silver-blue against the coffee-bronze of her skin.

"He wasn't doing anything, he just wanted a look." Kiara lifted her head to kiss Dylan. Curtis felt like crying. "Thanks again, babe, I just love it," Kiara said. "I'd better get going too. I've got to open this morning." She pushed back her chair and stood up. "Bye Curtis, see you next time."

Curtis managed to mumble something through numb lips.

Dylan walked Kiara to the front door. There was a brief exchange and then the familiar creak as the screen door opened. Curtis ran to the lounge room window and watched Kiara walk away down the garden path. Walk away with the Moami.

Not long after, Dylan jogged past his line of vision with Dad's surfboard under his arm. Curtis punched the striped couch cushions as hard as he could. *Punch*. That was for Dylan. *Whack*. That was for letting the Moami get away. *Sock*. That was for Dad leaving. *Thump*. That was for the stupid nickname. *Pound*. That was for—

"Hey, son-shine." He swung around to see his mother leaning against the arch between the kitchen and lounge room. Her faded cotton robe was knotted around her waist. She clutched a coffee mug.

"Hey, Mum." He was breathing hard.

"Everything okay? I think whatever those cushions did, they won't be doing it again in a hurry." She raised an eyebrow at him.

"Yeah, Mum. Everything's okay. I'm just…you know. How was work?" He changed the subject.

"I know." Mum gave him a gentle smile. "Work was fine. Old Mr Peters still thinks I'm the dancing girl he met at the Moulin Rouge in the forties." She sat down on the couch and patted the seat next to her. Curtis listened as she chatted away about the people she worked with, and the various patients she cared for. She paused every now and then to drink her coffee.

"Where's Dylan?" she asked, when she'd run out of stories.

"Gone for a surf," Curtis said. He didn't tell her that he'd taken Dad's board — *his* board.

"I heard the surf report on the radio. Supposed to be a pretty decent swell out there this morning." She gave him a long look.

"Yeah, apparently."

"Don't you miss it, Curtis?" She took his hand in hers and squeezed it.

"Of course I do, Mum. It's just, I can't. Not yet." His jaw ached as he fought back tears. How could he explain to her the chest-tightening cloak of dread that smothered him every time he imagined himself getting back into the water, when he couldn't even explain it to himself?

"You will, son-shine. When the time is right, you will."

"That's what Dr Mackenzie said."

"Well, he's right." She drained the last of her coffee. "Just remember, Curtis, there's no time limit on grief, and we all grieve in different ways. You, me and Dylan."

"I know, Mum," he said. "Now why don't you show me how to do the Can-Can like one of those dancing girls?" He poked her in the ribs.

"There you go, changing the subject again." Mum raised another eyebrow, but she was smiling too. "I'm going to have a shower. Can-Can indeed!" She stood up and crossed the room. As she left she turned and gave a high kick, her right leg flying out between the folds of her robe.

Curtis laughed. It felt good. He spent the rest of the morning helping Mum around the house. He washed the breakfast things and put them away. Emptied the bins and hung out a load of washing. The lawn needed mowing but Dylan could do that when he got back. It was one of the few things they seemed to agree upon these days — whatever it took to get Mum through they'd do. He knew that Dylan would never tell her he'd caused the bruises to his face, just as Dylan knew Curtis would never tell Mum about him taking Dad's board. It was an unspoken law between them — don't upset Mum.

Busying himself with the household chores helped him

keep his mind off what he was going to say to Navaya that afternoon, but as the sun changed position in the sky and the shadows drew longer, he knew he would have to make his way to the rock pool and deliver the news.

He told Mum he was going for a walk, and set out towards the beach. Would Navaya be angry? He recalled her mouth filled with pointed teeth, her strange emerald eyes, and all of a sudden wished he was headed anywhere but towards the rock pool. But he'd promised her his trust and he couldn't—wouldn't—renege on that.

CHAPTER 7

Curtis studied the surf as he walked along the beach. The barrels of the morning had given way to a gentle swell, and only a few long boards were out. The January storms would roll in any day now. The storms always brought a huge swell with them, whipping Midnight Cove's waters into churning, challenging conditions. Last year, he recalled, they'd had towering surf, with some waves past the second break reaching heights over six metres.

As he headed south towards the rocky shoreline of Midnight Bluff his heart skipped at the memory of shooting through tube after perfect tube. He wondered if Arax rode waves. Navaya had appeared as streamlined as a dolphin. She could probably —

"Hey." A voice pulled him from his thoughts. "Did you find what you were looking for?" It was the pale, freckled girl from yesterday afternoon. She didn't have her metal detector with her today.

"Oh, hi. Well, yes. No. I mean yes and no," Curtis said.

The girl tipped her head to one side. An expanse of sunhat moved with it. "So, just to clarify, is that a yes, or a no? Because it can, you know."

"Sorry?"

"The metal detector, it *can* detect cobalt."

"Oh, well it doesn't matter any —"

"Cobalt," she rattled off. "Is a chemical element with the symbol *Co*. Its atomic number is twenty-seven. It's found in the earth's crust, but only in its chemically combined form. The blue pigment of cobalt has been used since ancient times to—"

"Whoa." Curtis held up a hand. "What are you, like a human encyclopaedia or something?"

"I looked it up." The girl crossed her arms across her body. "I like to know stuff."

"Uh huh," Curtis said. He wasn't sure where to go with this conversation, and the afternoon shadows were getting longer. The girl opened her mouth again, but before she could launch into what the ancients did with blue pigment, Curtis cut her off.

"Well, nice seeing you again, but I've got to run." He turned on his heel.

"Why?"

"Sorry?"

"Why do you have to run?"

"I…" Curtis was taken aback. He hadn't expected to be questioned. "I just do," he said. "See ya." He started jogging towards Midnight Bluff.

When he reached the start of the rock pools, he glanced back. The beach was empty, save for a smattering of children in the distance trowelling a moat for their sandcastle with plastic spades. He traversed the rocky shelf as fast as he dared, leaping over smaller pools and scrambling around larger boulders. An easterly was blowing in across the ocean. It tousled his hair and carried with it a gently settling mist that tasted of salt when he licked his lips.

He passed the trapezoid rock. Dad's flowers flapped in the breeze as if waving him on. As he got closer to the deep rock pool with the curved rock ledge, his heart took up the frantic rhythm of a tribal drum. How was he going to explain to Navaya that the key she so desperately needed was now hanging around Kiara's neck? Perhaps she wouldn't be there. Perhaps he *had* just imagined her. Perhaps hallucinations were part of what Dr Mackenzie referred to when he spoke of the seven stages of grief. Perhaps—

There she was. Perched on the edge of the rock pool, her slender legs submerged to her knees. Her pearlescent skin glistened in the afternoon sun and he tingled with the same reality disconnect he'd felt when he saw Navaya the first time.

Navaya slipped into the rock pool and in one fast, fluid motion was on the other side in front of him. Water dripped from her coral headpiece. Her green eyes were brighter than he remembered.

"You came." Her watery voice was infused with gratitude. "I've searched the ocean floor, from the shelf to the slope to the sea bed, but there's no trace of the Moami. Tell me," her tone was pleading. "Tell me you found it on the shore."

Curtis saw the hope in her eyes and took a deep breath. "I'm sorry, Navaya. I didn't find your Moami." Navaya slumped down into the water, her head bowed. "But I do know who did," he added quickly. She looked up. "It was my brother."

"Brother of Curtis? Another son of Robert and Lori?"

"Yeah, Dylan."

"This is good news indeed. If Brother Dylan has the Moami, he will give it to you, and you will give it to me." Navaya's blowhole flapped rapidly.

"Um, yeah. It's not quite as simple as that," Curtis said. "You see, Dylan gave the Moami to Kiara."

"Kee-ah-ra?"

"Kiara is Dylan's girlfriend. He found it on the beach and gave it to her as a present."

"Then you must get it from girlfriend, Kiara."

"I tried this morning," Curtis said. "She…it got away."

Navaya paced the rock pool. She muttered to herself in her strange wind chime language of yesterday. Finally she stopped pacing and looked at Curtis. "Dylan and Kiara, they know nothing of me?"

"Of course not," Curtis said. "You told me not to tell anyone, and I promised."

"That's something, at least. More humans knowing of Araxie would only add to the trouble." Navaya stepped out of the rock pool showing the full extent of her body. She was taller than

Curtis remembered—at least as tall as Dylan—she stood a full head above him.

From behind a large, limpet-encrusted boulder came an audible gasp. Navaya whipped around. Curtis, startled, fell hard on his backside.

"Show yourself." Navaya's body tensed like a cat ready to pounce.

A large sunhat slowly emerged from behind the rock. A pair of grey eyes, wide with amazement, stared from the brim's shadow. It was the girl with the cinnamon hair.

CHAPTER 8

Navaya's lips peeled back. She hissed through her teeth, a dangerous noise that stopped the blood in his veins. She turned on Curtis.

"Deceitful human with false tongue." Her eyes flamed. "You said you could be trusted. You promised! And I believed you. But you told this girl. You brought her to see an Arax. Tried to hide her!"

"No, no. I didn't." He shrank from Navaya as she loomed over him, her face a mask of fury. "I don't know what she's doing here. I don't even know her. Never saw her in my life before yesterday." He swung to face the girl. "You followed me," he accused.

"Yes," the girl said. Her voice was barely more than a whisper. Her eyes swarmed all over Navaya.

"Why?"

"Because you were acting so mysterious with your yes, no, I dunno answers, and question dodging. I thought you must've been hiding something. It looks like you were." She stepped slowly out from behind the rock. Curtis watched in disbelief as she extended her hand towards Navaya in greeting. "Arax? Is that what your name is?"

"I am Navaya, daughter and protector of Araxie." Navaya disregarded the outstretched hand. "And a fool to trust humans."

"He didn't betray your trust. I followed him. I'm sorry if I've caused trouble."

Curtis snorted.

"It violates Araxie law for a human to see an Arax. And now two have seen me in half as many tides." Navaya shook her head. "Again I bring dishonour to my oath." She spat into the rock pool.

"I'm Morgan," the girl said. "I won't tell anyone about you. They wouldn't believe me anyway. Especially adults. They don't believe anything." She said to Curtis, "Does this have something to do with you asking about cobalt yesterday?"

Still in shock, he could only nod.

"I couldn't help but overhear," Morgan continued. "What you're looking for, the Moami? Maybe I can help get it back?"

Curtis snorted again.

Morgan ignored him and said to Navaya, "I swear your secret will be safe with me, and I'm really good at thinking things through. My dad says I have an analytical brain. That means I'm a good problem solver."

Navaya studied Morgan for a long time. "Well, Morgan," she said, "my problem is that it's crucial I recover the Moami. The danger of not having it outweighs the danger of human interaction. Maybe you can assist Curtis to retrieve the Moami from girlfriend Kiara."

"But, like I said," Curtis protested, "I don't even know her."

"I'm Morgan," Morgan said. "And you're Curtis." She stuck out her hand again. "Now we know each other."

"You're annoying," Curtis muttered, but he took her outstretched hand and gave it a quick shake.

"In your human mythology, the name Morgan means 'dweller of the sea'," Navaya said. "Your arrival could be viewed as a fortuitous omen."

"How do you know so much about us? I mean, a human has never even heard of an Arax—at least not that I'm aware—yet you seem to know about our ways. You even speak English," Morgan said.

"The human species is so young. Arax so old. But all creatures originally came from the sea," Navaya replied. She spread her hands out to where the waves crashed and foamed against their rocky barrier. The sun shone through the thin membrane between her fingers.

"Well, that's pretty enigmatic," Morgan whispered to Curtis. He shrugged.

"Why is the Moami so important?" Morgan asked. "If we're going to get it back, we need to know what it is."

Curtis couldn't help but be impressed at Morgan's straightforward nature. It was almost as if she encountered talking, human-like marine creatures every other day. He chimed in, "Morgan's right. We do need to know more about it. What's it a key to? You said yesterday the Glynts want what you have. What is it the Araxie have that's so important?"

"Glynts? What the heck's a Glynt?"

Curtis ignored her. "And why did you say humans are in danger as well?"

"What? Danger? What's a Glynt?" Morgan repeated.

Navaya let out a long sigh. It sounded like the breath of the ocean Curtis sometimes heard from his bedroom window.

"You are right. Sit. You will need to know the danger you face if you are to help Araxie. It's only fair." Navaya sat down on a smooth, flat rock and crossed her legs beneath her. Curtis and Morgan found seats on rocks nearby.

Morgan was the closest. Her eyes kept returning to the coral cap on Navaya's head. "Would you mind if I..." She reached out a hand to touch it. "Your head covering sure is weird." Navaya bared her teeth and Morgan snatched her hand back.

"Look who's talking," Navaya said, regarding Morgan's sun hat with distaste.

Curtis burst out laughing.

A trio of pelicans glided overhead, stark white wings stretched against a canvas of blue sky, and Navaya began to talk.

CHAPTER 9

"The Moami," Navaya began, "is a key. A long time ago, when the currents were still forming and your continents were a different shape, the Arax were pearl harvesters. Araxie seabeds were used for harvest. Our kind were farmers, and our pearls were prized not only for their green hue—"

"Green? I've never heard of a green pearl," Morgan said. "There's other colours of course. Pink and gold, and even black—they're the Tahitian ones. My mum has a pearl necklace, but they're boring cream ones—"

"Araxie pearls are green. The same colour as Arax eyes." Navaya's own eyes glittered as she glared at Morgan. "Do not interrupt."

"Sorry." Morgan shrank beneath her hat.

"As I was saying, our pearls were prized not only for their green hue, but also for their powers. Over time our hoards were plundered, our seabeds and molluscs destroyed, our people killed. Now there are only a few molluscs remaining from the original ancient harvest. They still produce pearls, but we have locked them away, safe from predators. They are kept in an underwater cave, deep down in a ravine. The entrance was sealed long ago. Only the Moami can open it."

"It was the Glynts who stole your pearls, wasn't it?" Curtis said. He leant forward, hands clasped between his knees. If what Navaya was saying was true, the ocean housed other races, other habitats, unseen and undetected. *Until now.*

"Yes, Glynts." Navaya spat again as if the name were a foul taste in her mouth.

"But why?" Curtis said. "What power do the pearls have?"

"To swallow a pearl gives the ability to walk and breathe on land for a limited time. This is what the Glynts want, to steal our pearls so they can move freely on land."

"Why would the Glynts want to come on to land?"

"To feed on humans."

Curtis' mouth dried up as if it had been filled with sand. Next to him he heard Morgan's sharp intake of breath and guessed she was feeling the same way.

"But, surely that's impossible," Morgan squeaked. "I mean, magic pearls I can just about swallow—no pun intended. But why would Glynts want to eat humans. Don't they like the taste of fish?"

Navaya shifted on her rocky seat as if delivering such news made her uncomfortable, but she held their gaping eyes, looking slowly from Morgan to Curtis as she continued. "Glynts believe the consumption of human flesh will carry the gene to breathe on land through to their future generations. They believe that eventually all Glynts will be able to breathe on land. The ability will have been bred into their offspring."

"You mean like evolution?" Morgan said. "I watched this show once about change within heritable traits of different species and—"

"Shut up," Curtis hissed.

"Evolution. Natural Selection," Navaya said. "Your kind has many names for it."

"So, let me get this straight. The pearls allow them to move on land for a short time? And they use that time to attack and kill humans?" Curtis couldn't bring himself to use the word eat. He was finding it difficult to breathe, as if he'd been punched hard in the stomach.

"Yes. But their folklore is wrong," Navaya said. "Imbibing human flesh will not enable Glynts to dwell on land, no matter how many generations they produce. Theirs is a primitive species. They are murderous savages fuelled by superstition and driven by greed and hunger for a power they do not deserve. They do not understand the lore of the ocean or the land."

"So, if the Glynts get the Moami, they'll have access to the cave where the pearls are kept?" said Curtis.

"Yes. The Arax would fight to protect the pearls, of course. But the Glynts are many, and Arax are few."

And yet, I've never seen one in all my time in the surf, Curtis mused. *Neither has anyone else, it seems.*

Navaya stood up. She looked to the horizon, her head held high. "I am a daughter and protector of Araxie, but also a descendant of the earliest pearl harvesters. It is my duty and destiny to protect the pearls." Her head dropped, along with her voice. "Although, I hardly deserve this honour now."

"Have the Glynts ever managed to come to land?" Curtis asked.

"Not for centuries. In the dark times when Araxie was marauded, they used the pearls they stole to move on land. They were dark times for humans too. Your history books will speak of people taken by unknown things, strange beasts that dwelt in rivers and forests. Impossible nameless creatures that struck fear into villages and turned talk to sorcery and witchcraft. The stories were not fallacies. They were the work of Glynts. Now, they get bolder in their quest for human flesh. Stories have been told that they have taken your kind — spear fishermen, abalone divers, even rock fishermen."

Curtis' heart fell down a flight of stairs. "Rock fishermen?" A wave of vertigo swayed and bent the day. He concentrated hard on the grains of sand at his feet, separating each tiny yellow-brown orb from the other until the dizziness passed.

"It has been said Glynts have timed the waves," Navaya said from a million miles away. "They ride incoming surges, snatch fishermen from rocks in their jaws, and carry them off with the backwash."

"You hear about so many rock fishing accidents," Morgan said. "People getting swept off ledges never to be seen again. Last year it was listed as one of the most dangerous sports in

Australia...but what if it's really Glynts?"

Curtis could see Morgan's mouth moving, but her words sounded distant and distorted as if his head was under water. A collage of images twisted across his mind—his father waving goodbye as he made his regular pilgrimage to fish from the rocks beneath Midnight Bluff; his mother calling out to take care as she always did; the *beat-beat-beat* of helicopters that filled the air during their fruitless search; a funeral without a body; a rock where plastic flowers kept a lonely vigil.

Navaya returned her gaze on them. Curtis struggled to keep his face neutral, but he felt her eyes linger on him. "You see now why it is crucial to get the Moami back?" she said.

Oh, Dad. Glynts. What if it was Glynts what if it was what if what...

"Curtis? Curtis? Did you hear what I said?"

"Huh?" He turned to Morgan.

"I said that we need to make a plan."

"Yeah, sure. A plan," Curtis said on auto pilot. *Dad oh dad were you taken by a Glynt is that what happened is that why they never found your body is that what happened is it was it did it Dad...*

"What do they look like?" Morgan asked.

"They are dwellers from the deepest seas, the abyss where sunlight never visits and little survives. Dark and sinuous, with a serpent's body. They have huge, hinged jaws studded with triple rows of long needle-like teeth that can open wider than the width of their body."

Curtis shivered in spite of the sun's warmth.

"That sounds a little like a viperfish," Morgan said. "My dad's got this old set of encyclopaedias, and one of them has a chapter called 'Monsters of the Depths'. Viperfish are in there. It's got pictures and everything. Sounds similar anyway."

"I know these viperfish you refer to," Navaya said, "although in our language we call them *ungh-charif*. Glynts are a little similar, I suppose. They are from the same depths at least, but Glynts are much, much larger."

A cloud moved across the sun turning the ocean dark and shadowy. Curtis had to get out of there. Be alone. "It's going to be sunset soon. I'd better get home, or Mum will kill me."

Morgan glanced up at the sky. "Yeah, me too. Why don't you give me your address, Curtis? I'll come over tomorrow and we can work on our plan."

"Sure," Curtis agreed. Anything to close the conversation. Right now he just wanted to be alone. He needed to think.

"So, we'll report back tomorrow afternoon. Same time, same place," Morgan said.

As they turned back toward Midnight Cove, Navaya called after them, "Be very careful, and remember there is one sure way to know if a Glynt is close."

"What's that?" Morgan shouted. The easterly had whipped up again and she held her sunhat down as the wind fought to steal it from her head.

"Their smell. They are creatures of vile stench." And with a graceful leap, she cleared the rock ledge and disappeared beneath the waves.

CHAPTER 10

The next day was raining, a light drizzle that arrived in a sheet of slate-grey cloud, and added to the humidity. Curtis slouched about the house. There was nothing on television but he flicked through the channels anyway. It gave him a cover while he considered what Navaya had said about Glynts taking rock fishermen.

"Turn it off if there's nothing on, son-shine. You can always help me with the ironing if you're looking for something to do." Mum passed the lounge room carrying a laundry basket over-spilling with towels and sheets.

Curtis pulled a face. "Love to, Mum, but I've got a friend coming over soon."

"Oh? Is Tyler back already?"

"Nah, not 'til just before school starts back. Same with Lachlan. It's a new friend. A girl."

"Oh?" Mum put down the basket with interest.

"It's not like *that*, Mum. Just a girl I met on the beach." Curtis couldn't even begin to think about Morgan the way he thought about Kiara. "Don't go getting yourself worked up."

"Cheeky devil," Mum said.

"What's that? Curtis' got a girlfriend?" Dylan stuck his head round the archway.

Curtis rolled his eyes. "No, moron, I don't have a girlfriend."

"And you never will."

"Shut up, Dylan."

"Don't start arguing already, you two. Here, Dylan, you

can take this." She shoved the basket of washing into his arms and steered him towards the laundry. Dylan groaned, but took the basket and allowed Mum to herd him along.

Several hours later, there was a knock at the door. "I'll get it," said Mum, and before he had a chance to say anything, she was trotting down the hallway. He couldn't help but smile at her interception, it was just so *Mum*.

"Let me take that umbrella. It hasn't let up all day has it? Come in, this way. Curtis is around somewhere. Curtis? Curtis? Your little friend is here."

Little friend? Geez, Mum.

Morgan trailed behind Mum as she led her down the hall and into the kitchen. Mum had deployed her secret weapon—interrogation in the guise of small talk. "So, you and your family have just moved to Midnight Cove? How nice. Where from? Any brothers or sisters? No. Just you. And your parents, they like it here so far? Oh, I see, so your father works from home? An architect—how nice. And you'll be starting school this year…"

Morgan caught sight of Curtis and raised her eyebrows. Curtis shrugged and smiled an apology.

"So can I get you two anything? Orange juice? There's some biscuits in the cupboard. I could—"

"Mum, we're fine. Seriously."

Mum looked from Curtis to Morgan and back to Curtis again. A silence hung heavy in the air. "Okay then, well you don't need me hanging around," Mum said. "I'm off to work soon anyway. It was nice to meet you Morgan."

"You too, Mrs Creed."

"Oh, call me Lori. All the kids call me Lori."

"Bye, Mum," Curtis said.

Morgan watched her leave the room, amusement lit her usually serious eyes. She turned to Curtis. "Awkward."

Curtis laughed. "I know. Poor old Mum, she's all right. She's always reading something into nothing and gets all weird. Come on, we'll go to my room so we can talk in private."

He led Morgan to his bedroom and half closed the door. Morgan sat down at the old desk where he did his homework and looked about. Without her sunhat, her hair hung long and straight down her back. It made her look even thinner, like she had the bones of a tiny bird. He watched her eyes travel about his room, taking in the surfing posters, unmade bed, and piles of clothing that bulged from his dresser.

"Sorry, it's a bit of a mess," Curtis said. He kicked a pile of tatty-leaved surfing magazines under his bed.

"It's fine," Morgan said. She'd caught sight of his trophy shelf and stood up for a better look. Without asking, she picked each one up and read the engraved inscription. She let out a long, low whistle. "Wow, Curtis. You must be an awesome surfer. Look at all your trophies."

"Used to be," Curtis muttered. He plucked at the loose threads of his doona cover.

"What do you mean? This one's only from last year." She held out a trophy with a marble base. It was topped with a little gold effigy of a surfer.

"I don't surf anymore," he said.

"Why not?" Morgan looked at him in surprise. "If I was that good at something, I wouldn't just give it up."

"I didn't just give it up." A rush of anger surged through him. Why did everyone always assume he just gave up?

"Sorry," Morgan said. She quickly replaced the trophy on the shelf and sat back down.

Curtis immediately wished he hadn't snapped at her. It wasn't her fault. "Nah, I'm sorry," he said. "Didn't mean to bite your head off. It's just— "

"Did something happen?" Morgan asked. "Did you hurt yourself or something and you can't surf anymore?"

"Yeah, something happened," Curtis said. His cheeks puffed out as he expelled a long breath. He may as well tell her. It couldn't be any crazier than the things she'd heard in the last twenty-four hours. Besides, there seemed to be something in Morgan's programming that allowed her to bring calmness to the most extraordinary situations. He'd seen it in her the first time she met Navaya, the crazy-confident way she'd stuck out her hand in greeting.

"When Dad died—," he began.

"Oh, I'm so sorry," Morgan's eyes softened into grey pools of sympathy. "I didn't know."

"It's okay. Why would you?" Curtis said. "Anyway, when Dad died, I surfed more than ever. The ocean was the only place that I felt I could really be myself. It—I dunno—it seemed to understand how I felt. Does that make sense?" He stopped, feeling heat colour his cheeks. He looked sideways at Morgan, but she wasn't laughing. She nodded at him to go on.

"Anyway, one day I was out surfing the usual break, when I saw a fin cut through the water right next to me. A large shadow passed under my board. I thought it was a shark and started shouting and screaming for everyone to get out the water. I paddled like mad for shore. It wasn't until I reached the sand that I realised everyone was still in the surf. It was just a pod of dolphins swimming past. It happens all the time."

"I'd be pretty scared if I thought a shark was in the water with me," Morgan said.

Curtis brushed the flop of hair out of his eyes. "Thing is, sharks *are* out there. It's just part of surfing. We're playing in their back yard. I've seen one before. Never had that effect on me though. Anyway, my brother, Dylan, and his mates thought it was a huge joke and they've called me Shark Crumb ever since."

"Shark Crumb?"

"Yeah, as in they reckon a grommet like me would be no more than a crumb to a shark. Pretty dumb, huh? I hate it. Thing is, I haven't been able to go back in the surf since. It's like a mental block or something. I just can't bring myself to do it. Every time I try it feels like my heart's gonna jump right out of my body. I get all sweaty and dizzy, and my chest feels like there's a weight so heavy on it I can hardly breathe." He stopped, surprised. He'd never talked so much about it to anyone. For once Morgan hadn't interrupted.

"Wow," she said. "It sounds like some kind of anxiety or panic disorder or something. Did you know twenty percent of people experience a mental health issue every year? That's a fact. I don't think people realise how common it is to—"

Curtis held up his hands. "Okay, enough Dr Mackenzie."

"Who's Dr Mackenzie?"

"The doctor Mum sent me to see when Dad died and all this surfing trouble started. You're right, though. He reckons it's anxiety triggered by grief. Something to do with how we deal with psychological trauma. You sound just like him." He hunched over and did his best Dr Mackenzie impression. "So, you see, Curtis, there's no shame in what you are experiencing. One in five people experience a mental health issue of some degree in their lifetime."

Morgan laughed. "Sorry, everyone tells me I talk too much. I can't help it."

"I've noticed." Curtis crossed his legs under him and laughed too. It felt good to talk to someone that didn't know him; couldn't judge him. "I guess I'll eventually get over it… whatever *it* really is. In the meantime I'm stuck with this stupid nickname."

"You *will* get over it, Curtis." Morgan said. "You will, when the time is right."

"Okay, now you sound like Mum." Curtis threw a pillow at her. She ducked and lobbed it back.

"So, I guess when you do get back to surfing, you'll be thinking about Glynts now instead of sharks," Morgan said, serious now.

Curtis was just about to answer when a head swung around the door. "Is this your girlfriend, Shark Crumb?" It was Dylan.

Curtis sighed. "Dylan, Morgan. Morgan, Dylan."

"I'm not his girlfriend," Morgan scoffed.

"Red head, feisty!" Dylan laughed.

"My hair is not red," Morgan said. "It's copper. Did you know that red hair only occurs naturally in about two percent of the population? So real red hair is not as widespread as you think. In fact—"

"Yeah, whatever," Dylan cut her off. He said to Curtis, "Kiara and I are hitting the surf. Catch you later."

"Hi, Curtis." Kiara's face joined Dylan's around the doorframe. The Moami was around her neck.

"Hi, Kiara." Curtis willed Morgan to catch sight of the Moami. He gave an exaggerated cough and rubbed his throat.

"Hi Morgan, I'm Kiara. It's nice to see Curtis with a friend." Curtis' blush matched the colour of Morgan's hair and he fumbled for something to say.

"Hello," Morgan said. "I love your necklace."

Smart girl, thought Curtis. She'd spotted the Moami.

"Thank you. Dylan gave it to me yesterday. Isn't it awesome? Look at the gorgeous blue stones in it. Blue's my favourite colour." Kiara held the pendant aloft. Curtis thought the cobalt was a good match for her eyes.

"Come on, babe, let's wax up." Dylan said. "Catch you later, Shark Crumb. Later, Red. Don't do anything I wouldn't do."

"Get out of my room, Dylan."

"Not in it." His laughter faded down the hallway.

"Stop calling him that awful name." Kiara's voice was the last thing they heard before the whine of the screen door announced their departure.

"Is he always like that?" Morgan asked.

"Yep. Pretty much. Since Dad died anyway. Before that he was really cool." He changed the subject. "So, you saw the Moami."

"It's beautiful," Morgan said.

"You're the one with the analytical brain. How are we going to get it back?"

"We could always just ask her for it," Morgan said. "That would be the obvious thing."

"Are you nuts? And tell her about Navaya and everything. We promised Navaya we wouldn't do that. Besides, look how cross she was when she thought I'd spilled my guts."

"I know, I know." Morgan sighed. "To be honest this whole thing is so surreal, it feels like a dream."

"Agreed," Curtis said. "Dunno about you, but it's not every day I get caught up in quests to retrieve keys to ancient caves with green pearls. Or hear about land-walking viperfish with a taste for human flesh." He shook his head slowly. "You know, I'm actually really glad you followed me. Now that you've seen Navaya I can finally tell myself I'm not going crazy."

"Maybe we both are," Morgan said. "Let's see if we can find out anything online. Surely we can't be the only two people in the world to have ever seen an Arax or heard of a Glynt." She leaned across Curtis' desk and snapped on his computer. Next to it was a framed picture of Curtis and his dad. In it they were standing on the front lawn beside the hibiscus bush. Dad had his arm thrown about Curtis' shoulder and they were laughing into each other's faces. He remembered the day Mum had taken it—it was her fourth attempt at capturing a nice father and son picture, and she was getting cross because Dad kept pulling faces to make him laugh.

"Is this your Dad?" Morgan asked.

"Yep."

"How did he die? Was it cancer or a car accident or something?"

"No. He died in a rock fishing accident. He was swept from the rocks by a wave and drowned at sea. They never found his body."

Morgan swung around. "Oh, Curtis," she breathed. "You don't think…" She trailed off, unable to finish the question Curtis knew she wanted to ask.

He nodded. Their silence was broken by the computer's screen whirring to life.

lackety clack. Morgan's fingers flew across the keyboard. G-l-y-n-t-s she typed into the search engine and pressed Enter.

Curtis pulled a seat up next to her and watched as the screen threw up a number of blue-linked listings. There was nothing for Glynts. *No search results listed.* The search engine informed them in its tidy little font, then suggested: *Try again for glints.*

Morgan shrugged and punched in Glints. A number of company names filtered down the screen, accompanied by the Merriam-Webster dictionary definition: *Glint: to shine in small bright flashes; to glance off an object; to appear briefly or faintly.*

Of primitive, foul-smelling, flesh-devouring serpents from the deep sea, there was no mention.

Morgan tried again with Arax and Araxie. Again, there was the usual smattering of business-based listings, but nothing at all to do with Navaya's species. No matter what combination of spelling or keywords Morgan tried—*Aryx, Aracks, Glintz, Glyntz, smelly viperfish, Moami, green pearls*—it was as if the internet had never heard of either Arax or Glynts.

"I thought we might have at least gotten some clues as to how to get the Moami back, or learn more about Glynts. I'm normally really good at computer research," Morgan said. She looked despondent, as if let down by an old friend.

"It's just like Navaya said. No one has ever heard of Glynts or Arax, or the land, or kingdom or whatever it is, of Araxie," Curtis said. "Even when people were attacked by Glynts in the past, they thought it was something else, remember?"

All of a sudden, a terrible thought gripped Curtis. Dylan's words wailed like a siren through his mind. *Kiara and I are hitting the surf. Catch you later.*

Kiara would be in the ocean, wearing the Moami. What if Glynts attacked her to get at it? What if they—

He jumped up and seized Morgan's arm, dragging her from the chair. "Come on, Morgan. Let's go."

"What? Where? I haven't finished—"

"To the beach. We have to stop her. Glynts. The Moami." Curtis swore as he tripped over the side of his bed.

"Of course. I'm so stupid." Morgan smacked her forehead with her palm before tearing down the hallway after Curtis.

They hit the road at a run and pelted towards the beach. A mist of rain clung to the air like an eerie shroud, and Curtis clung to the possibility that they weren't too late.

CHAPTER 11

A small crowd gathered near the shore, and Curtis elbowed his way through the throng, Morgan close behind.

"Hold this tight against her shoulder." A lifeguard, his yellow and red cap plastered to his head from the rain, threw a wadded up towel to Dylan. "The pressure will help stem the flow of blood."

Kiara sat on her knees, grey-wet sand beneath her. A deep gash sliced her left bicep. Blood trickled down her arm in a slow rivulet, staining her blue bathing suit with rust coloured blotches. Dylan knelt down beside her. When he pressed the towel against the wound a rosette of blood bloomed through the fabric. Kiara winced at the pressure.

"Sorry, babe," Dylan said. He was wincing himself, and in spite of the fact it was Dylan, Curtis felt for him. Kiara too.

"S'okay. I'm sure it's worse than it looks." Kiara attempted a weak laugh.

"Actually, you're pretty lucky," said the lifeguard. He closed the first aid kit that was open on the sand. "That's about all I can do. It's not too serious, but you're going to need some stitches in that. I'll radio and get a buggy down here. Get you off to hospital." The lifeguard jogged back to his tower.

Kiara groaned.

"Don't worry, Kiara. Stitches don't hurt that bad. It's more the thought of them." Curtis' words came out in a tumble of relief. Kiara was wounded, sure, but it was just a cut, it looked like she was going to be okay. The Moami was still safely around her neck.

"Where did you two come from all of a sudden?" Dylan looked from Curtis to Morgan, then shifted position on the sand to better apply pressure to Kiara's wound.

Curtis ignored him. "What happened, Kiara? What attacked you?"

Kiara looked at him in surprise. "What do you mean? Nothing attacked me." She laughed. This time it sounded more like the old Kiara.

"Well, what caused that then?" Morgan said. Rain dripped from the tip of her finger as she pointed at Kiara's arm.

"It was the fin of my board. It was the weirdest thing. I was lining up for a pretty decent wave, was almost on it, when all of a sudden it was like my board was pushed up and out from under me. That's the only way I can explain it. Anyway, I was already committed to the wave and got smashed in the barrel. My board came down on top of me and I got sliced by the fin."

Morgan elbowed Curtis. He nodded. The cut did look clean, as if sliced by something knife-sharp. It didn't strike him as the sort of wound that triple rows of fangs might inflict. He imagined that would be much more of a mess. But what about what she'd said about her board being pushed? It sounded like something had deliberately tried to remove her from it.

"I'll tell you something else strange," Kiara said. "When I was getting dumped it felt like something was tugging at my necklace, pulling on it hard. I couldn't see anything, of course, it was like a washing machine under there. It was just so weird—like the sea had grown hands or something." She rubbed her neck at the memory.

"Geez," Dylan moved her hand away. An ugly blue blemish had already started to appear on the side of Kiara's neck where the whale hide had been pulled taut against it.

Curtis and Morgan exchanged a look. "You didn't happen to notice anything else unusual out there, did you?" Curtis said. "Like—oh, I dunno—a strange smell or anything?"

"Uh, no," Kiara said. "That's a pretty random question. Why?"

The lifeguard trotted back just then, and Curtis threw him a silent word of thanks. He wasn't sure how to answer Kiara.

"Buggy's on its way. I've radioed ahead to the hospital. They'll have you stitched up in no time. Come on, let's get you up." The blood flow had stemmed. The lifeguard taped the towel to Kiara's arm and together he and Dylan eased her up off the sand. She cradled her left elbow with her right hand. To Curtis she looked like a beautiful bird with a damaged wing.

The crowd, along with the rain, had dissipated by the time the buggy came into view. It approached from the northern end of Midnight Cove, whipping up a fine spray from the wet sand as it raced across the beach.

The two lifeguards loaded Kiara into the back, while Dylan hoisted their boards onto the roof. He squeezed in next to her. "What a shame you're going to have to miss The Yell tonight," he said.

"Fat chance," Kiara said. "I wouldn't miss it for anything. It's just a few stitches, I'll be fine."

"Why don't we just wait and see how—"

"*Dylan*. I'm going," Kiara cut him off.

The buggy's motorised drone drowned out their conversation as it headed back off up the beach.

"**W**hat was that all about?" Morgan asked. She gathered her hair into a rope and twisted it over her shoulder to wring the water out.

"I dunno," Curtis said, "but I don't like the sound of it. The cut caused by her fin, I can believe that. Seen it before. But did you see that bruising on her neck? Something was pulling real hard on the Moami."

"They didn't get it though."

"A Glynt for sure, I'd say."

"Yes. But no smell."

"Maybe she couldn't smell it because she was under water.

Or perhaps they smell different to Arax than they do to us. What Navaya might think of as a really bad smell, might not smell bad to us."

"That's true," said Morgan. She rubbed her chin.

Curtis glanced at his watch. "Speaking of Navaya, we'd better get moving if we're gonna be at the rock pool on time."

"Navaya's not going to be happy with this latest update," Morgan said. She fell into pace beside Curtis as they headed south towards Midnight Bluff. "Firstly, we still don't have the Moami, and now it seems the Glynts are on to it."

"Navaya," Curtis said seriously, "is going to freak."

CHAPTER 12

Navaya stormed up and down the rock pool. Every now and then she kicked at strands of seaweed that caught about her legs. Curtis could hear her muttering to herself in Araxie. It didn't sound much like his grandmother's wind chimes this time, more like the sound the last of the bath water makes as it's sucked down the plughole.

"I was this close." She changed to English when she caught sight of them. "*This close.*" She held her thumb and index finger apart. Her hand shook causing the fin that ran the length of her arm to flutter.

"Uh, this close to what?" Curtis asked. He and Morgan stopped near the rock where Morgan had concealed herself — was it only yesterday? He didn't feel comfortable getting too close to Navaya when she was so angry. She reminded him of a pacing tiger.

"The Moami. I had it right in my hand. I pulled as hard as I could, but a wave turned everything upside down and I felt it slip away. By then I was too close to shore. Too dangerous, humans everywhere. *This close.*" Navaya stamped her foot into the water. The spray reached Curtis and Morgan.

"It was you?" Morgan said. She used her forearm to dry her face. "Not a Glynt?"

"Me? Me what?" Navaya looked up, distracted from her outburst.

Curtis emerged from behind the rock. "*You* pushed Kiara

off her board?" He didn't know whether to be relieved or angry.

"I felt the Moami's call and followed its voice. I saw the Moami. I went to reclaim the Moami." Navaya spoke slowly using the explaining-to-children voice Curtis remembered from when she'd first described the Moami to him.

"I understand, Navaya, but Kiara got really hurt. Her neck's all bruised up and her arm's cut so bad from the fin of her board that she's going to need stitches."

"That is unfortunate, but it could have been worse. A lot worse. Glynts can also hear the call of the Moami. Here, perhaps this will help with her cut?" Navaya ran her hands along the submerged rock face until she found an anemone. She scraped it free and held it out to Curtis.

"What's that for?" Morgan said, wrinkling her nose.

"Never mind, long story. Thanks, Navaya, but I don't think it will help. What do you mean *the call* of the Moami?" Curtis asked.

"Vibrations. They travel through water mostly. The Moami carries the life force of the pearls within. There are those who can feel it, and there are those who cannot. Arax and Glynt both feel it. Some other creatures too—dolphins, whales, others." She held the anemone under water until it had affixed itself back on to its rock.

Curtis' eyes widened. "I felt it too," he said. "In the kitchen, when I was trying to get the Moami. As soon as I touched it, it was like some kind of electric shock ran through me. I didn't know what to think at the time. What? Why are you looking at me like that?"

Navaya was staring at him as if seeing him for the first time, her head to one side. Her green eyes grew fire-bright.

Curtis looked to Morgan, but she just shrugged.

"When you helped free me, you touched me. I thought I felt it then," Navaya said. "But I didn't think...it was all so quick, and I was in pain and distress."

"Felt what?" Curtis said.

"Touch me now." Navaya held out her hand. Curtis' arms

felt frozen at his sides. He didn't want to touch her. She looked like she might grab him and not let go.

"Touch me," Navaya repeated. It was a command.

"Touch her," Morgan hissed from behind.

Curtis stepped forward and slowly extended his arm as if to shake hands. Navaya seized his hand. Her palm was as smooth and supple as eel skin, the membrane between her fingers felt like soft leather. The pearlescent sheen of her skin contrasted sharply against his own deep tan. She closed her eyes for a moment, then released his hand.

"You have it," she murmured. She shook her head in disbelief. "A human? In all my cycles of the moon—"

"Have what?" Curtis interrupted.

"You have a gift, Curtis, son of Robert and Lori. You hear the ocean. You understand its voice."

"What does that mean?" Curtis said. But in his heart he felt he might already know. The ocean had been a part of him for as long as he could remember. It was where—up until the last year—he felt most comfortable, most at home, the most complete.

"Do I have it?" Morgan rushed forward and thrust her hand into Navaya's.

"No. You do not. Despite the implication of your name." Navaya dropped Morgan's hand.

Morgan looked disappointed, but not surprised.

"So what do I do with this gift?" Curtis asked. He wondered if there had been a mistake. These days it felt like he was already drowning in a riptide every time he thought about entering the water.

"That is not for me to know. If the ocean has allowed you to access her soul, then that's her bidding. It will serve you well, of that I have no doubt. But how it is used, that I can't tell you. I have never known a human to hear the voice of the ocean before."

"So, why can the Glynts hear the—what did you say it was—voice of the ocean?" Morgan asked.

"They do not have the same gift. True, they can hear the life force of the pearls, which is why they can pick up the vibrations of the Moami. It's why they were able to track me down and attack me. You recall I said they don't understand the lore of the ocean and the lore of the land. That is the true gift, to be privy to the ocean's wisdom." Navaya spread her arms wide as if to embrace the sea beyond. The earlier rain had caused the ocean to whip and foam, and the incoming waves cresting the rocky ledges of Midnight Bluff now seemed to Curtis to carry something much weightier.

"What does that mean, exactly? The ocean's wisdom?" He cupped his hand and dipped it into the rock pool. He let the water run through his fingers, feeling for anything different—a vibration, a message, a voice. There was nothing but the cool familiarity of water against his skin as it trickled back into the pool, stirring the sand beneath.

"Now is not the time to explain, even if I did have the answer to your question. The gift is different for all creatures." Navaya placed her hands on Curtis' shoulders. "For now, the best thing is to try to be worthy of your gift."

"But how do I do that, if I don't even know what it means."

"I'm sure you'll know when the time is right." Navaya's lips peeled back revealing her pointed teeth. Curtis realised it was an attempt at a smile. It looked comical on her usually solemn face. Behind him Morgan stifled a giggle. He stretched his own lips back to return it, but his smile felt strained. *A gift. I have a gift. The ocean's wisdom. How can I be worthy of something I don't understand?*

"Look! Look! Did you see that?" Morgan's voice was shrill with excitement. She had clambered up onto a large rock and was looking out to sea. "I've never seen one so big."

"What is it?" Curtis scrambled up the rock next to her. Navaya hauled herself up to the curved ledge of the rock pool, chin-up style, and peered over.

"A spout. The biggest one I've ever seen. It was huge. A whale. Dunno what sort though. It's not Humpback season, they're not due up this way until at least July." Morgan leant forward scanning the ocean. "There it is again. Did you see that?"

Curtis let out a long, low whistle. There was no way he could have missed it. About a kilometre offshore, a huge jet of water blasted upward. The fountain reached fifteen, maybe twenty metres, and then it was gone.

"Did you see it?"

"Sure did," said Curtis. "It was like a fountain of water coming back down."

Morgan nudged him hard in the ribs with her bony elbow. "It's not water, silly. It's air. A whale's spout is condensed water vapour, like the steam you see when you breathe out on a cold day. Don't you know anything?"

"Not as much as you, obviously." Curtis elbowed her back.

"Ow. I wonder what sort of whale it is."

"Not whale. Arax," Navaya said.

"An Arax did that?" Morgan said, her eyes round.

"It is a traditional Araxie signal," Navaya explained, lowering herself back into the rock pool. "If we need to communicate with others from a distance. It is like—" she paused as if searching for the right word. "It is like when humans send up a flare."

"There are other Arax out there right now?" Curtis asked. His eyes searched back and forth across the ocean. It was hard to fix on anything with the rise and fall of the swell.

"My people are gathering. The Glynts know the Moami is missing. If it falls into their hands, it will mean war." Navaya let out a long sigh. "My fault. All my fault."

"But Kiara still has the Moami. We saw it around her neck. It's safe on land," Curtis said.

"Safe!" Navaya spat into the rock pool. "The Moami will never be safe until it is back in Araxie." She slipped into the water and glided around the rock pool in miserable circles. Her blowhole flapped slowly, making the loops and whirls that encircled it elongate and contract.

"We will get it back, Navaya. We will," Curtis said. An idea had started to grow legs in his mind.

Navaya lifted her head. Water cascaded down the coral cladding and along the length of her nose. "You mean well but time is running out. If we can't get the Moami back and return to Araxie, there will be a battle. One that we might not win. And it will be all my fault." She sank back down into the rock pool.

Curtis waded in and placed his hands on her shoulders like she had done to him moments ago. Should he ask her if it was possible a Glynt had killed his father? Would she even know? The words were almost out of his mouth, but her face was so etched with the misery of her failings, that what came out instead was, "You are Navaya, daughter and protector of Araxie. Don't be so hard on yourself. If there are so many Glynts, you did well to protect your pearls all these—uh—moon cycles." He felt a bit like his mum giving a pep talk, but Navaya had looked up at least. He continued, "Everyone needs help sometimes. Morgan and I will get the Moami back. Won't we, Morgan?" He looked over his shoulder to Morgan for support.

"You bet." Morgan said, although her voice didn't match the enthusiasm of her words.

"You mean well, but you don't understand." Navaya sat up. "It's not just the Moami. I've also brought danger and dishonour to my people. Revealing myself to humans, telling you our secrets. I have put humankind in danger too. You should never have seen me. And again today, I risked discovery by swimming close to humans, close to shore. And now, the Arax are closer than they've ever been to the coastline because of my errors. Any human could have seen that spout."

"If they did, they probably would have thought it was a whale, like Morgan. Besides, it's a pretty miserable day," Curtis offered. "There's not too many people out because of the rain." What Navaya said was true though. The spout could have been seen by a fishing boat far off shore. Anyone high up on the Bluff could have seen it if they were looking out to sea at the right time. "Anyway," he continued, "if it wasn't for a human, you could still be trapped and bleeding in the rock pool, so some good came of it."

"There is truth in your words," Navaya said, "but I must go to my people now. We have much to discuss. They will be expecting news of the Moami. I will not be able to give them the news they need. I won't return here again. Araxie needs me. I must stay close to my kinfolk. You have tried to help, but without success, so now—"

"Tell your people you will have the Moami by morning," Curtis said. The idea that had been sprouting legs was now fully formed and galloping across his mind.

Morgan gasped. "Curtis, what are you saying? You can't make a promise like that."

"Navaya, meet me here at dawn. I will have the Moami. Then you and your people can go home." He offered his hand to Navaya. She took it and he helped her to her feet. "You just need to trust me, okay?"

Navaya looked at Curtis, then out to the ocean where the spout had blown. Her eyes came back to rest on him. "I've trusted you this far, and you've given me no cause to feel that trust has been misplaced. Very well, one last time, Curtis. What can it matter now? I will be here at dawn."

"And I will have the Moami. I swear on my father," Curtis said.

Navaya looked at him a moment longer and then she was gone, diving again from the ledge to disappear into the ocean's whitewash with her usual agile grace.

"Curtis, what did you say that for?" Morgan was practically turning inside out. "You just made a promise you don't even know you can keep."

"Chill out, Morgan. I've got a plan. We're going to get the Moami back tonight."

CHAPTER 13

"So what's the big plan?" Morgan said. The wet sand sucked at their feet as they trudged along the beach, Midnight Bluff's rugged cliffs growing distant behind them. "How are you going to get the Moami?"

"Not me," Curtis said. He looked at Morgan and grinned. "*You.*"

"What? *Me?*" Morgan stopped in her tracks. The wind whipped her hair about her face. She swished it back to reveal eyes narrowed with suspicion.

"Yep," Curtis said. "Tonight at The Yell."

"What on Earth is The Yell? Is that the same thing Kiara was talking about earlier on the beach. Said she didn't want to miss it, or something?"

"The Swell Yell," Curtis explained. "It happens the second weekend every January. Locals just call it The Yell. It's been happening for as long as I can remember. Mum and Dad used to take us when we were kids. It's mostly just teenagers that go now though."

"But what's it all about? What happens—a whole lot of yelling?"

Curtis laughed. "Yeah, there's a bit of yelling involved. It's kind of a festival, I suppose, to welcome in the storm season. The idea is the more noise you make, the larger the swell will be. Midnight Cove has wicked surf all through January and February, and local legend goes that the storm gods are flattered with the attention they get during The Yell and surfers are rewarded with awesome conditions."

"So, it happens down on the beach?" Morgan asked.

"Nah, it's held on the banks of the estuary. That way, everyone can set up a picnic or whatever. Some people bring barbeques and music. When it gets close to sunset, a surfboard gets set on fire and pushed out into the estuary. Someone different is chosen every year to launch it. As it starts floating out to sea everyone starts making as much noise as they can—yelling, cheering, some people bring drums, or pots and pans to crash together—anything goes. It's really cool." As Curtis talked he realised he was looking forward to The Yell in spite of what needed to be done. It had always been one of his favourite events on the Midnight Cove calendar—back when he was still surfing at least.

"Okay, so what does The Yell have to do with me and the Moami?" Morgan said.

"Well, we already know Kiara is going to be there. She wouldn't miss it even if she had to have her arm amputated. We'll be there too. We're gonna strike up conversation, and then you ask if you can have a closer look at the Moami. She'll take it off to give it to you; you give it to me and I run like hell."

"How on Earth do you know that she's going to give it to me?" Morgan said.

"'Cause girls do that sort of thing all the time," Curtis said. "They're always ooh-ing and aah-ing over each other's clothes and jewellery and stuff. Kiara won't say no, trust me. She even gave it to me to look at when Dylan first gave it to her. I had the Moami right in my hand. I was *this close*." Curtis held his thumb and forefinger apart and did his best imitation of Navaya's watery voice.

Morgan didn't laugh. "So what happens after you run off and I'm just left there? The girl that stole Kiara's prized necklace?"

"Um, I didn't really get that far. Besides, it won't be you that will 'steal' it. Technically, that will be me."

"I don't like it, Curtis. I don't like it one bit."

"It's not ideal." Curtis raised his hands palm up. "If you can come up with a better plan by tonight though, I'm all ears."

Morgan ground the toe of her sandal into the sand as if digging for inspiration, then let out a long sigh. "I guess it's the best shot we've got if you're going to get it back to Navaya by morning." They turned towards the sand dunes to exit the beach. "The Swell Yell it is."

"Thanks Morgan, I owe you one."

"I'm not doing it just for you, you know." Morgan said. "There's so much more at stake. If what Navaya says is true, can you imagine if the Glynts got their hands on the pearls? Started coming on land? Started eating...," she trailed off with a shudder. "Curtis, we're not just doing this for us or to restore Navaya's honour, it's bigger than all of us."

Curtis stopped. She was right. The gravity of what they were doing—the bigger picture—slammed him with the force of a rogue wave. *Dad, oh Dad.* He looked out across the ocean, and for a moment the sea seemed to roil and writhe with black serpentine bodies. He blinked and it was gone.

Their feet sank deep into the still wet sand of the dunes and they continued on in silence, tackling the steep incline. They had almost crested the largest dune and the level grassland of the foreshore was in view when Morgan said quietly, "Curtis? What do I wear?"

"What do you wear?" Curtis repeated. "I dunno, wear whatever you want to wear. Clothes are always a good start." He shook his head. Girls were pretty weird sometimes. The sandy path between the dunes gave way to dirt. "Come on," he said.

But Morgan had stopped. Curtis couldn't see her face, it was hidden behind her hair, but when she talked her voice wavered. "It's alright for you. You know everyone. You've lived here all your life. I'm always the new girl. I never fit in anywhere and this time it's going to be worse than ever." She sat down with her back to him, facing out to sea.

Curtis stood for a moment unsure of what to do, then walked back and sat down next to her. The wet sand soaking through the bottom of his shorts felt cool against his skin. "What do you mean it's going to be worse than ever?"

"School starts in a few weeks and I don't know anyone."

"Well, you'll get to meet a heap of kids tonight," Curtis said brightly. "Then you'll know a few other faces when you start, besides mine of course."

"Yeah, everyone will know *my* face. Here comes the new girl that stole Kiara's necklace."

"They'll forget, Morgan. Besides, just blame it on me. I'm the one who's going to run off with it."

"Oh, don't you understand *anything*?"

He shrank from her ferocity.

"Look at me, Curtis. Look at me. I'm the skinny girl with the pale skin, ranga hair and freckles in a town filled with bikini-clad surfer chicks. My skin burns to a crisp after a few minutes in the sun. The other girls are all tanned and beachy. Once, just once, I want to fit in and not feel like such a freak every time we move."

"You move around a lot, huh?" Curtis wasn't sure how to comfort Morgan. He hadn't known her long, but she didn't seem like the sort of girl that would go for all that huggy stuff. He leaned over and attempted an awkward shoulder pat, but Morgan shrugged it off and launched afresh.

"We're always moving. Dad gets these ideas in his head that a new location will give him inspiration for his architectural drawings, and then we're off again. The mountains, the rainforest, the Outback. This time he thinks a 'coastal view'" — her fingers drew quotation marks in the air — "is going to help with his latest project. And every time I have to start all over again. A new town, a new school, new friends. It sucks." Morgan picked up a hunk of driftwood and flung it as far as she could.

"Yeah, that would be really tough," Curtis said. He imagined how it would feel to be continuously uprooted. He thought of how the anemone withdrew its tentacles when Navaya pulled it from the water; torn from its home, recoiling from its strange new environment.

"It's just so hard to make friends being me. People think I'm too serious, too smart, a show off. They call me a know-it-all, say I talk too much—"

"Well, you could work on that a *little*," Curtis said, and immediately regretted his lame attempt at humour as Morgan's mouth bowed and sagged.

"I can't help being different." She pulled her knees to her chest and wrapped her arms around them.

"But that's what makes you so rad," Curtis said, and realised he meant it. "You're one of the coolest girls I've ever met. You know random stuff that most adults wouldn't even know—that's so cool. You're really smart, and brave. You weren't even scared the first time you met Navaya, or to touch her. Who cares what you look like when you're all that kind of awesome?"

"You seriously think I'm cool?" Morgan held his gaze as if to gauge his sincerity.

"I sure do," Curtis said. "Let's see." He began to tick things off his fingers. "The first time I met you, you were using a metal detector. *A metal detector.* That scores pretty high on the coolometer, in a geeky kind of way. Then you followed me around the Bluff. Hardly anyone ever goes around the Bluff—it's just so dangerous, especially after the…well, Dad's accident, if that's even what it was. Then you hardly batted an eyelid when you saw Navaya—it's like you've just been waiting your whole life for someone from Araxie to show up. You know all about freaky stuff like cobalt and viperfish and whale spouts and panic disorder. Heck, you even had a crack at Dylan about the difference between red hair. Shall I go on?" He glanced sideways at Morgan.

"I guess if you put it like that, I am pretty cool, right?" Morgan was smiling now.

"The coolest," Curtis agreed. "Morgan, don't worry about what you're going to wear to The Yell, just go with whatever makes you feel comfortable. It's not a dressy thing, just a bunch of kids getting together at the estuary."

Morgan stood up and brushed sand from the seat of her

pants. "Okay, what time shall I meet you then?"

"We want to get there before the burning board gets launched so we've got time to put Operation Moami into action. Why don't you meet me outside the kiosk next to the car park by the estuary at about half past four? You can tell your folks you'll be back in time for dinner."

"Okay."

They exited the beach in single file, the narrow path flanked by orange-pink bursts of lantana bushes. A bush turkey scratched and swaggered in the undergrowth beside them. "I'll see you soon, then," Morgan said, as they turned towards their separate homes. "Oh, and Curtis?"

"Yes."

"When I give you the Moami, you better run like hell, okay? I'm not going through all this for the plan to fail."

"Oh, I will. Running's kind of my thing. I've had a lot of practice these holidays. You could say I'm gifted."

"Looks like you've got more than one gift then," Morgan called over her shoulder.

Her words brought back the exchange he'd had with Navaya. Was it true? Did he really have some sort of gift? He remembered what he'd felt when his hand closed about the Moami. A deep thrumming vibration that infiltrated every cell in his body. 'Be worthy of your gift,' Navaya had said. And when he'd asked how to do that, she'd replied that he'd know when the time was right. What the heck did that mean?

The sky rumbled overhead as if adding its own thoughts to those that swirled around his head. Thick grey clouds linked arms across the sky, muting the afternoon light. The storms were right on target this year, Curtis thought, as he turned into Jacaranda Street. This one looked like it might even kick in before The Swell Yell.

CHAPTER 14

Showered and refreshed, Curtis leant against the brickwork of the kiosk. He checked his watch. Morgan should be along shortly. He hadn't seen Dylan at home, he must have already left for the estuary. Mum wasn't there either, but she'd stuck another note under the pineapple magnet. *I've pulled the night shift, lucky me! Have a great time at The Yell*, she'd written. *Don't stay out too late, the weather is about to turn. Please try not to wake me in the morning.* She'd finished with a row of kisses.

She was right about the weather. A Southerly had been building steadily offshore all afternoon. Fronds on overhead palm trees slapped playfully at each other in the breeze. From the nearby parkland and banks of the estuary, a large crowd had already started to assemble. The sounds of The Yell carried on the breeze and he smiled at the familiar noises — the crack of leather as a cricket bat met a ball, the hypnotic rhythm of multiple bongos, the strum of guitars, and the happy cacophony of numerous radios and speakers adding their own backbeat to the gathering.

The aroma of sausages frying alongside onions evoked other memories — Dad snapping at Mum with the tongs by their old brick barbeque in the back yard. Mum's shriek-laugh as she fended off the tongs, while he and Dylan chased each other around the Hills Hoist.

"Well, look who's here. If it isn't Shark Crumb." Dylan rounded the corner of the kiosk. Jordo and Blake were with him. They clowned around, pulling each other into headlocks then rubbing the top of the other's head with their knuckles.

"Let's give Shark Crumb a noogie, too," Jordo said.

"Yeah, want a noogie, Shark Crumb?" Blake made a lunge at Curtis while Jordo struck up the theme music from *Jaws*. "*Da-da. Da-da. Dun-dun-dun-da, dun-dun-dun-DA!*" He carved his hand through the air in the shape of a fin for emphasis.

Curtis rolled his eyes. A few days ago, he probably would've run. But a lot had happened in the past few days that made Blake and Jordo, and even Dylan's antics, seem insignificant.

Across the kiosk's car park, he could see Morgan approaching through the Norfolk Island Pines that grew in tall ranks along and around the estuary. He didn't want her to face the taunts of Dylan and his cronies too. "Gotta run, losers." He neatly sidestepped Dylan, wove between Jordo and Blake, and jogged across the car park to meet her. Behind him the catcalls and whistles faded and melded with the sounds of The Yell.

Morgan had smoothed her hair off her face and woven it into a long braid that hung down one shoulder. She was dressed practically in jeans and a t-shirt; a pair of runners completed the outfit. "Operation Moami chic." She smiled.

Curtis laughed. "Come on, let's go see if we can find Kiara. Dylan and his drongo mates are here, so she's bound to be around somewhere."

"What if the cut was worse than it looked and she wasn't able to come?" Morgan said.

"Nah, you heard her. Kiara wouldn't miss The Yell for anything." They picked their way through the scores of people that flocked to the estuary. Little clusters had started to form sporadically across the park by way of picnic blankets surrounded by eskies, tripod barbeques, and foldout chairs. Bags of potato chips shared blanket space with plastic plates of pink watermelon wedges and bottles of soft drink. Some of the older kids drank beer from bottles cocooned in styrene holders.

The encroaching sunset filtered through the tall trunks of the pine trees, bathing The Yell in shadows that danced and flickered as if in time with the bongos' rhythm.

It was slow going moving from group to group scanning for Kiara, as there were many faces to greet and acknowledge. "G'day Curtis." "Haven't seen you in the surf all Summer." "How's your mum?" "Surf's gonna be epic tomorrow if this storm kicks in." "Catch you at school in a few weeks." "Where've you been hiding, dude?"

After the low profile he'd kept since the whole Shark Crumb thing started up, it felt good to see so many familiar faces. He did his best to field them all, bumping fists, answering the easy questions, and evading ones about surfing. He introduced Morgan to as many people as he could.

"I'll never remember all these names." Morgan said as they left another group, and made their way to the crowds gathered on the banks of the estuary. "Half of Midnight Cove must be here. Did you know there's a scientifically proven way to remember people's names? It's something to do with picking a physical feature that really stands out and then trying to associate that with the person's name. I'll have to read up on—"

"There she is." Curtis grabbed Morgan's arm and pointed towards a trio of girls seated on a blanket overlooking the estuary. Kiara's left arm was swathed in white bandage between her elbow and her shoulder. Her long hair bounced in the wind offering glimpses of the Moami adorning her neck. His heart picked up the rhythm of the drums—*beat-throb beat-throb*. They were really going to do this.

"So, what now?" Morgan said. "We just go say hi, and strike up conversation?" She twisted her braid between thin fingers.

"Yeah, I guess so," Curtis said. He could already feel the wool knitting itself across his throat at the thought of talking to Kiara. Why did she always have this effect on him? At least Dylan wasn't there. Yet. He took a deep breath. It wasn't too late to change his mind. They could always just melt back into the park, join a group, enjoy The Yell. But then he thought of Navaya's face, the glimmer of hope that had crossed her green eyes like a ripple of wind across the ocean's surface. Besides, he'd made her a promise. He'd sworn it on his father.

"Come on. We'll just have to play this one by ear." His heartbeat went from percussion to trip hammer as they neared the girls. Morgan didn't look any more relaxed than he felt. She chewed her lip and twisted her braid furiously.

"Give us a look, Kiara," said a girl with cropped bleached hair. Curtis recognised her as one of Kiara's workmates from Curlz, the surf store.

"Okay," Kiara said. She folded her long brown legs beneath her and began unwinding her bandage. Her girlfriends huddled around her.

"Aren't you worried about scarring?" Curtis heard the other one ask.

"Nah, it's such a smooth cut. Doc said the sharper the cut, the cleaner it heals." This was greeted by a chorus of "Ew's" from the girls.

Curtis and Morgan were behind them now. There was no turning back. Curtis attempted to speak, but the words caught in his treacherous throat and nothing but a strangled cough came out. Morgan raised an eyebrow at him.

"Oh, hi Curtis." Kiara swivelled on the blanket to see what had made the noise. "Girls, you know Curtis, Dylan's brother? And this is…it's Morgan, right?" Morgan nodded. Curtis blushed. The girls giggled.

A thousand things he would like to say to Kiara crossed his mind, but nothing appropriate would pass his lips. A million years passed. The girls blinked at them expectantly, and Kiara smiled kindly.

"We wanted to know how your arm was," Morgan blurted out, and Curtis could have kissed her.

"Yeah, how many stitches did you need?" Curtis' mouth finally decided to cooperate. He threw Morgan a grateful look. She gave him her other eyebrow.

"Only twelve," Kiara said. "Have a squiz if you want." She patted the blanket, and that was it. They had an in. Curtis inspected the row of neat stitches that laddered her arm. The sutures resembled fishing line and as Kiara coiled the bandage back around her arm, Curtis recalled how Navaya's ankle had oozed and gaped the day he found her.

Morgan turned out to be Operation Moami's best asset. She took to her position on the blanket with great strategy, charming the girls with questions about hairstyles and flattering them by asking their advice on everything a girl might need to know about Midnight Cove.

As the daylight faded, pairs of rainbow lorikeets came home to roost in the giant Norfolk Pines. Their screeching added another dimension of noise to The Yell, and Curtis knew that soon the surfboard ceremony would begin. He nudged Morgan with his foot. *Hurry up*, he mouthed at her.

Morgan deftly steered the conversation to jewellery and Curtis looked about for a clear path to make a break for it when he finally had the Moami. It was going to be tricky with so many obstacles blocking the normally uncrowded parkland. He could see Dylan off to the right, kicking a football around with Blake and Jordo and some of the other high school seniors. He'd run to the left instead. Through the cluster of pandanus, back around the kiosk and follow the back streets until he felt the coast was clear. He wished he'd thought to hide his push-bike somewhere to speed up his getaway.

"Would you mind if I had a look at the beautiful necklace Dylan gave you?" Morgan was saying, and Curtis snapped his attention back to the girls.

"Sure," Kiara said. She eased it from around her neck, and handed it to Morgan. "I love it so much. I'm so glad I didn't lose it in the surf today. She touched her neck, wincing at the angry bruises left by Navaya's assault.

She was just about to drop the pendant in Morgan's outstretched palm, when the sound of a gong overshadowed all other noise. It reverberated through the dusk. The Swell Yell had begun. Bongos became more urgent and a static charge of excitement filled the air. Scores of people pushed forward to line the banks of the estuary for a better view of the ceremony.

And then Dylan was there, holding an old board under one arm. "Surprise, babe," he yelled. "You've been chosen to launch this year's burning board. Considering the injury you copped in the surf today, it's only fitting." The crowd whooped and cheered their approval. Kiara's eyes were vivid with delight, and she allowed Dylan to haul her to her feet.

"Here, let me hold that for you," Morgan said, and before Kiara could reply she quickly reached out and palmed the Moami. Kiara was borne away from the blanket and down to the water's edge in a swirl of laughter and cheering.

Morgan had the Moami. The pendant lay in her palm all silver and cobalt. The whale leather cord coiled neatly around it. She met Curtis' eyes and silently asked the question. *Now?*

Curtis gave Morgan a quick thumbs up and rechecked his exit route. It didn't matter so much now as all but a few of the picnickers now lined the bank of the estuary, and attention was firmly on the unfolding ceremony. The waning sun lit up the rolling surf beyond the estuary's mouth before it disappeared below the horizon.

And then everything seemed to happen at once.

The surfboard floated on the surface of the water while the little nest of newspaper and kindling was placed atop it and lit. Kiara waded into the estuary until the water lapped at the frayed hem of her denim shorts. She watched as two boys fanned life into the fire. Smoke gave way to little yellow flames that framed Kiara's face in warm shadows.

"It's time," yelled an older boy with bleached-out dreadlocks. "Let the Swell Yell begin!"

Kiara grasped the edges of the board and pushed it out into the estuary. It bobbed on the surface, bouncing on the ripples the Southerly had whipped up. As the current ushered it slowly out towards the mouth of the estuary and the ocean beyond, the crowd saw it off with an almighty ruckus. Midnight Cove echoed with cheers and chants, banging and beating, yelling and swelling, and somewhere in the middle of all the hubbub, Curtis heard someone say, "Phwoar, what's that smell? Dude, did you let one off?"

Something unpleasant scampered in the pit of Curtis' stomach. He knew he should be far away with the Moami by now, but something felt very wrong. He signalled to Morgan to follow and elbowed his way to the front of the crowd. He could smell it now too. The estuary seemed to fill with the pungent stench of rotting vegetables.

"No. Oh no. Curtis, you don't think—" Morgan was beside him. His eyes scanned the water, but it was hard to see anything unusual between the choppy wavelets. The pink-grey gloom of dusk cast strange shadows across the estuary, playing tricks on his eyes. Was that an unusual shape moving towards the banks? He squinted at the water. Yes, there was something unnatural out there, cutting through the water with unnerving speed.

All around him now people were holding their noses and making retching noises at the ghastly smell. Kiara was still in the water. She'd wrapped her long hair around her face to block her nose. A few others were in the shallows too. Dylan, the dreadlocked boy, and a handful of others that had helped with the fire.

A short distance away the water broke, then rose and fell as great inky-black coils closed in on Kiara and the others. The sinewy body was fronted by a blunt diamond-shaped head. It had to be a Glynt. There was a Glynt in Midnight Cove's estuary—hungry for flesh—and he and Morgan were the only ones who knew.

"Do you see it?" Curtis pointed to the middle of the estuary where the massive head had just dropped beneath the surface. Morgan peered in the direction of his index finger. Her sharp intake of breath confirmed it. The remainder of the Glynt's ugly serpentine body undulated through the water like a perverted giant eel. "What do we do, Curtis? What do we do?"

The horrific stench combined with the amplified noise from the crowd made it hard to think. Curtis kept his eyes on the Glynt. The next time it surfaced, it locked in on the embankment where Kiara and the others were still thigh-deep in the water. Even from the shore he could make out the oil slick gleam of its eyes. The Glynt angled its head like a rudder and gunned directly at Kiara. The crowd was so worked up by the foul smell, it seemed he and Morgan were the only ones who could see it. Curtis had to get Kiara and the others to safety.

"Get out of the water!" he screamed. "Get out of the water!" He waved his arms in the air, the universal distress signal.

"Get out of the water!" Morgan took up his cry, but it was no use. Their voices were lost in the din of the crowd. And then Curtis cupped his hands and bellowed the only thing he could think of. "Shark! Get out of the water! Shark!"

It worked. The electric word rolled through the crowd like a tsunami.

"Shark."

"There's a shark in the water."

"Get out of there, you guys."

Amid the frantic splashing from Kiara and the others in their haste to get out of the water, it was hard to make out what was happening. Curtis saw Dylan lunge for Kiara's outstretched hand. He tugged her to shore and they collapsed on the safety of the grassy embankment. Between the foaming whitewash, Curtis glimpsed a huge jaw unhinge to reveal a nightmare view of curved needle-like teeth. The Glynt glided past where Kiara's legs had been a moment before. Its jaws snapped, closing on nothing, before disappearing back under the surface with a flick of ugly black tail.

"What was that? Did you see that tail?" someone yelled.

"The shark? Was it a shark?"

"Dude, that was like the biggest eel, I've ever seen."

"Not an eel. That was a sting ray."

"So, whatever it was, it wasn't a shark?"

"No way, bro. Never seen a shark like that before."

Opinion raged about what had been seen in the estuary, and Morgan tugged Curtis' sleeve. "They're safe. It's time. Take the Moami and get out of here. No one will notice among all this commotion." She pressed it into his palm. The moment it touched his skin his body thrummed. It was as if the Moami was a living, breathing thing joining its energy with his, until his whole body pulsed with it.

"Go, Curtis, run. Tell Navaya I said goodbye. I won't be able to meet you at the rock pool in the morning, there's no way my parents would let me out that early without getting suspicious that I was up to something."

"That's okay. You've been amazing. There's no way I could've done it without you, Morgan." On impulse he gave her a quick hug.

"Go," Morgan said, and gave him a friendly shove. "And, good luck."

Curtis hung the Moami around his neck for safekeeping and ran. As he ducked and wove between the crowd snatches of conversation reached his ears:

"What *was* that thing?"

"I heard reports there was a crazy big whale spout spotted from the Bluff this afternoon too. Could be related."

"Definitely wasn't a shark. Who yelled shark?"

Me, Curtis thought, as he ran across the grassland towards the kiosk. Fruit bats chattered in overhead trees as if laughing at him. Of course it had to be me, Shark Crumb. When word got out that it was he who'd yelled shark, he was sure it would just add to Dylan's repertoire.

Still, it had worked, hadn't it? So it was worth it. He had saved Kiara, Dylan and the others too. But it had been a near thing. Although he hadn't managed to get a close look at the Glynt, it was worse than any creature he'd pictured in his dreams.

The Moami bounced against his chest as he ran. It felt warm and comforting as if it knew it was going home. He matched his breathing to the rhythm of its energy, and as he sped through the car park and raced around the kiosk, he felt he could run forever.

CHAPTER 15

The house was dark when he got home. Mum was at work, and Dylan would probably be at The Yell for some time. He locked his bedroom door and collapsed on his bed. When his heart rate finally started to slow, he held the Moami up on its cord for closer inspection. It was so beautiful, so intricate, with its swirls and loops of blue against gunmetal grey.

"Just a few more hours, Moami, and you'll be going home with Navaya." He smiled in anticipation of Navaya's reaction. Outside, the wind picked up tempo carrying the boom of the surf. It was one of his favourite sounds and had lulled him to sleep many a night during the early days when Dad died. Nights when he'd stared at the ceiling for hours with burning eyes, trapped beneath a thick blanket of grief.

He didn't think he'd be able to sleep tonight either, especially with the image of the Glynt's impossible jaw etched on his brain, but light rain drumming its fingertips on the tin roof joined the wind and ocean's lullaby, and the next thing he heard was the jarring creak of the fly screen door.

His eyes snapped open and he fumbled on his overflowing bedside table for his clock radio. The ghost-green display informed him it was 4:12am. Mum must have come home from her shift. That meant dawn would break shortly. He couldn't believe he had slept and sent a silent prayer of thanks to Dylan of all people. Mum had been pestering him for weeks to fix the squeaky door, but he'd never gotten around to it.

Curtis pulled on a pair of shorts and put an ear against the door. He listened to the sounds of the house, waiting for the coast to clear before he made his escape. There was the fridge door opening and closing, the sound of the kitchen tap as Mum rinsed her glass, the creak of floorboards as she made her way down the hall. At last came the whisper-snick of her bedroom door closing. He waited a few more minutes to be absolutely sure she wasn't coming back out, and stole out of his room. He hopped along the hallway, dodging places he knew the floorboards would give him away. He exited from the laundry door at the back of the house as silent as a ninja.

He crossed the lawn, wet from the overnight showers, and sped down Jacaranda Street towards the beach. All around him the dying of the night gave way to harbingers of the new day. Hidden birds nattered and warbled their morning chorus; the heady scent of jasmine and frangipani mingled with the salt-wet smell of the ocean, and the horizon glowed with golden warmth as the sun competed for space in a sky crowded with thunderheads.

Curtis enjoyed the feel of the Moami bouncing against his chest as he jogged along the beach towards the Bluff. The gale had picked up speed, but the wind was at his back and he ran close to shore where the wet sand was at its firmest. The impending storm cell had littered the usually pristine beach with all manner of detritus—logs and driftwood, palm fronds and husks, long strands of russet seaweed, shards of plastic, a lone sandshoe. With each tidal surge, more debris was pushed up the foam-flecked sand. Curtis marvelled at the huge swell. Whitecaps foamed and furied, and out past the headland some of the waves were easily ten metre boomers.

At last sand gave way to rocky shelf and he scrambled around the Bluff as quickly as he could. The rocks were slick with kelp and slippery wet. All around him powerful waves boomed and crashed over the rocks, sending their spray skywards. Curtis pushed wet hair from his eyes, ignoring the salt sting. He splashed through swollen rock pools that seemed to have taken on a tidal pull of their own. He was going to make it on time. The day was lightening rapidly, but he was so close now.

There was Dad's rock, almost hidden but for a flutter of coloured plastic petals, grimly holding their own under the pounding of the surf. On a day like today it was easy to see how someone could be swept from the rocks. But was it an accident? He couldn't get the image of the Glynt's terrible snapping jaw from his head. Did those teeth close around his father's leg? His waist? Did they sink into his arm before snatching him away into the roiling sea? Did he drown before he was eaten? *Oh, Dad, was it an accident? Please let it have been an accident!* He realised he'd probably never know. "This one's for you, Dad," he muttered. He squeezed the Moami hard as if to transfer all the anger and helplessness he felt.

Navaya was waiting. The rock pool was under siege from crashing waves, sending streams of water over the curved ledge. Curtis grinned when he saw her. He pulled the Moami from his shirt and held the pendant up for her to see. Navaya's emerald eyes flamed triumphantly and her lips peeled back in a grin of her own. "*Mushalat Cur-tis breh-sonay cin, Moami,*" she bubbled. The sun's rays breeched the horizon and her pearlescent skin reflected back its beauty.

"Huh?" Curtis laughed. "English, Navaya."

"You did it, Curtis. You did it. You saved the Moami." Navaya skipped across the rock pool like a little girl, gossamer fins fluttering from her calves and elbows. Curtis laughed again at her un-Navayalike behaviour.

"I made a promise, didn't I?" he said. He took the Moami from around his neck and held it out to Navaya. She reached for it—

Too late. Too late.

The stench of rotting vegetables filled the air. Another wave crashed over the rocks. Through the wall of water Curtis saw a darkly sinister shape writhing and twisting. It crashed down with the wave and landed in the rock pool with an almighty splash.

The Glynt was between him and Navaya. He let out a yell of shock and snatched his hand back to hide the Moami. The Glynt rose up on its body, spring-like. Curtis could see it clearly now. While it had the general shape of an eel, four paddle-like appendages sprouted from the sides of its elastic body. The appendages were fringed with suction cups, rather like a gecko's foot. Feet? The Glynt had feet. Curtis' stomach skittered like a crab across the sand. The Glynt swung its head back and forth looking first at him, then Navaya, then back to him. Its cold black eyes reminded him of a snake about to strike. The morning took on an unreal quality.

The Glynt's body tensed, ready to spring. The enormous jaw unhinged. Rows of long, deadly teeth in an overcrowded mouth. Curtis saw it all as if watching a film play out in slow motion. The dreadful stench. Waves crashing all about him. Navaya screaming...

Navaya screaming. What was she screaming?

"Run, Curtis!"

Reality's tentacles hauled him back just as the Glynt launched itself. It landed with a wet smack, half in-half out of the rock pool. He scooted back just in time. The Glynt snapped at where his foot had been a nanosecond before. It hauled itself up for a fresh attack just as Navaya landed on its back with a guttural war cry.

"Run!" she commanded.

Curtis hesitated. He couldn't leave Navaya, but he knew she'd want him to protect the Moami.

"Remember the signal, Curtis. Remember the signal." Navaya's eyes blazed into his. *"Now run."*

The last thing he saw before he turned and fled was her teeth sinking into the blue-black flesh behind the Glynt's broad head. A sinewy coil ensnared her body and the rock pool churned with the thrashing and clashing of battle.

CHAPTER 16

Curtis couldn't remember the journey back to the beach. It was all *rock-slip, splash-graze, heart-beat, salt-spray, sand-stagger.*

Sand. Stagger. The beach beneath him. He raised a hand to his chest. The Moami was still there, he could feel it beneath his t-shirt. For a terrible moment he thought its vibration had died, but then he felt it. The gentle thrum helped ease the shock of the Glynt's attack.

What was he going to do now? Was Navaya hurt? Dead? He couldn't see how she could have defeated something of such ferocity. And those teeth—he shuddered at the memory. Where Navaya's were sharp and short and neat, the Glynt's teeth were crammed into its nightmare mouth like rows of deadly scythes. He sank down on the beach, and watched the surf roll in while he collected himself. Mighty sets surged forward like a herd of wild, white brumbies. Only the bravest, most experienced surfer would take on waves like that, he thought, or the craziest. He couldn't remember the last time he'd seen such challenging conditions. How did the Arax cope out there when the surf was whipped into such a frenzy? His train of thought brought Navaya's words back. What was it she'd said before she screamed at him to run? *Remember the signal.* She'd told him to remember the signal. Of course. He jumped up and raced towards the track that would lead him to the top of Midnight Bluff.

The path at the end of the beach started at the base of the

cliff. It wound steeply up to the lookout at the highest point of Midnight Cove, giving sweeping views of the Pacific Ocean and miles of coastline that stretched in a golden arc to the north and south. Curtis ran up the rocky track that had been carved out between pandanus palms and patches of lantana. The wind wasn't at his back this time. It rioted around the cliff face, buffeting him with great gusts. It made progress slow, and by the time the track reached the steep turn towards the summit where sets of wooden steps had been installed for ease of passage, his lungs screamed with effort and his legs felt as if weights were attached to them.

One foot in front of the other, holding the handrail for balance. Four steps to go, three steps, two, one. He reached the top and bulleted across to the wooden platform built on the edge of the Bluff that served as the lookout. It was still too early for anyone to be about, but he knew that it wouldn't take long for people to arrive, keen to view the mighty surf that was battering the Cove. He hoped he was right about Navaya's words. *Please be alive, please be alive.* He breathed deeply to steady his heart rate, leant on the wooden railing and rested his chin on his hands. He fixed his eyes to the horizon and waited.

And there it was. A huge jet of water burst from the surface and shot skyward like a blown fire hydrant. It was higher still than the one he'd seen with Morgan, and he let out a whoop to rival the wind. It was the signal all right; the Arax equivalent of a flare.

Curtis made careful note of where the spout had appeared. He bent as far over the lookout's railing as he dared, scouring the rocks far below at the base of the Bluff. He settled on a distinctive cluster of copper-tinged lava boulders as his landmark. It was hard to judge from the booming surf, but he estimated Navaya was no more than three hundred metres off shore.

There was only one thing to be done, but if he stopped to think about it he'd never do it. He sped towards the road at the rear of the Bluff that snaked its way along the coastline.

It would be a quicker route home than using the stairs and beach. It was all downhill this time. He passed a few surfers coming in the opposite direction making the pilgrimage to the lookout.

"G'day, you're up early. Whad'ya do, wet the bed?" one of them said good-naturedly.

"Bitchin' surf," Curtis returned, as he flew past them. He was glad they hadn't been there a few minutes earlier to witness the spout.

The early morning sun took on a filtered quality as the storm that had been threatening for the past twenty-four hours rolled in. Green-grey clouds united at the horizon and drew themselves like a static sheet across the sky. Curtis' feet pounded along the Esplanade and turned into Jacaranda Street just as an eerie electric calm settled across Midnight Cove. It was going to be a doozy of a storm, but Curtis couldn't think about that now. He had a job to do.

He skirted around the house as quietly as he could. It was dark and quiet. Mum would still be asleep, hopefully Dylan too. He approached the wooden rack that hung from a wall under the carport. Dad had constructed it one rainy autumn. It held all their surfboards neatly lined up beneath each other. His own board, untouched for months, waited like a neglected friend. It was still waxed from the last time he'd used it, but this wasn't a job for it. His eyes turned to the thruster, Dad's board. *My board*, he corrected himself. It was the only board that was up to the job.

But what if you're not up to the job, Shark Crumb? a cruel voice in his mind whispered. *Shut up. Just shut up*, he told it, and swung the board out of the rack. His wetsuit hung on a hook nearby, another neglected friend. He pulled it on and zipped it up, the familiar tightness encasing his torso. Beneath the suit's neoprene the Moami pressed firmly against his chest.

With the thruster under his arm, he trotted back down the driveway. *I'm scared, Dad. Be with me. I need you.* He glanced up at the darkening sky. *And keep that storm at bay just a little bit longer, okay Dad?*

The cruel voice inside his head piped up. *You haven't surfed for months, pussy. You'll be lucky to make it ten metres offshore, let alone get around the Bluff. Glynts are going to smell you. You're wearing the Moami, you fool. What if Navaya's not even there? She's probably lying in a pool of violet blood right now —*

"Where the bloody hell do you think you're going?" Dylan's voice was incredulous.

Curtis swung around. Dylan stood on the front porch staring at Curtis as if he was an alien.

"Promise you won't tell Mum," was all Curtis said. He turned and raced away.

"Curtis! Curtis, wait. You'll get murdered out there," Dylan called after him, but he tuned out his brother's words and kept running.

The first thunder crack came as he reached the shore. It boomed right over his head, singeing the air and causing the hairs on the back of his neck to rise. Then the rain fell. Fat, sub-tropical drops that thudded on the sand, sporadically at first, then quickly building momentum.

The storm engulfed the morning. Curtis' heart was a bird in a cage, frantically beating its wings. The water, churlish with brown foam surged around his legs as he bent to fasten the Velcro of the ankle strap. The tell-tale dizziness he'd felt the last few times he'd attempted to enter the water clouded his mind. Sweat prickled his brow when he straightened up and looked out to sea. Clouds had stolen the sunlight, turning the water black as it churned and raged in the storm's grip. The waves rolling into Midnight Cove were immense, but out around the Bluff where he'd seen Navaya's signal, they towered like giants he'd only ever seen between the safe, glossy pages of his surfing magazines.

The heaviness in his chest was exacerbated by the tightness of his wetsuit. What had felt familiar and comforting only ten minutes prior, now felt constrictive and claustrophobic. But he had to go out there, he had to do it. He'd come this far and there was no turning back.

He angled the thruster's nose towards the horizon, and

forced his legs to move from the safety of the shore. One step, two steps, sand beneath his feet, his heart in his mouth. And then he was down on the board paddling. His arms swept through the water, propelling him out into the ocean proper. He rose and fell with the swell, paddling into waves, cresting them when he could. At other times he duck dived, sinking the nose of the board beneath the water just before a wave broke over him to emerge from the other side paddling furiously to avoid being washed back towards the shore.

His paddling became mechanical as instinct kicked in. He lost count of the number of times he dived, lying flat on his board to create the least resistance. Beneath the surface the water was turbulent, the shadows and light played tricks with his mind. Was that a sleek inky hide that flashed past on his right? Did a cold, dead eye stare into his as he propelled upwards? Curtis tried to ignore the feeling that any second curved, needle-like teeth were going to sink into his thigh, his torso, his neck. He could feel the Moami throb beneath the wetsuit. *They'll sense it. They'll come for me. Like the one in the rock pool,* his mind clamoured.

He caught a lull in the waves and looked back towards the shore to see how far he'd come. He'd made it out past the first break and was at the point where he needed to round the headland to reach where he'd seen Navaya's signal. His eyes searched out the red-tinged lava boulders he'd chosen as his landmark, but the teeming rain made visibility difficult. It stung his neck, his head, his face, each drop striking his skin like a miniature bullet. At last his eyes locked on the boulders. He still had to make it a couple of hundred metres around the rocky coastline. He took a deep breath and paddled onwards to where monster waves ruled the ocean. *Please be there, Navaya. Please be there,* he begged silently. He'd expended so much energy paddling out this far his arms now felt like they were moving through wet cement.

Something long and dark wrapped around his arm. He screamed and flailed, but it clung tight, emerging from the water like a dark streamer. It was seaweed. Just a strand of seaweed that had caught around his arm. Curtis shook it free, almost sobbing with relief. The burst of adrenalin spurred him on, and he slowly crested the headland, navigating by snatched glances at the lava rocks whenever the swell allowed him a glimpse of the shore.

He was almost there. The ocean was ruthless and relentless, with more water and power in her barrels than Curtis had ever known, but he was almost there. The huge waves towered all around him, and he gripped the rails of the board tightly with both hands, ducking as best he could with each oncoming face. And then, beneath the surface as a huge wall of water passed over him, suddenly she was there. Navaya arrowed through the water, a living torpedo, the filmy fins on her arms and legs now engaged like rudders.

Curtis broke the surface, and she popped up beside him, her coral-clad head close to his. She rested an arm on his board. "You came," was all she said. But her eyes communicated a galaxy of unspoken words.

"Yeah," he said. "I came."

"Duck," Navaya commanded. And they were back beneath the sea as another wave passed over them.

When they returned to the surface, Navaya wasn't the only Arax that bobbed among the whitecaps. Curtis guessed there were at least twenty others. They were similar in feature to her, all with head coverings of varying lengths and protection, and brilliant green eyes. Some had skin and fins of differing hue, or facial features that distinguished them as distinctly male or female. A broader nose and forehead on that one on the left, and what could only be a beard framing the face of that one, and over there two females that blinked at him beneath long, moss-like lashes.

"My people," Navaya said. And then it was time to duck again. They all dived in unison and Curtis caught glimpses of the same tattoo that ringed Navaya's blowhole on the others.

"Here," Curtis said, when they broke surface. He fumbled for the Moami. "I've got to get back. This surf's gonna hammer me." He sat astride his board in order to unzip his wetsuit enough to free the pendant.

As the Moami came into view the Arax gave voice as one to a single, beautiful note. Their harmony filled the air with a sweetness that reached deep into his soul, and for a moment everything around him ceased to exist. The howl of the wind and the ocean, the rain striking his face, the relentless walls of water, and the threat of Glynts. Lost in the peace of the Araxie song, nothing else mattered. At last it dwindled, the combined voices growing fainter until the echo of the note was carried away across the ocean.

"My kinfolk say thank you, Curtis, son of Robert and Lori. Our song expresses our gratitude and recognises your gift. The story of your bravery will be retold and remembered among the Arax."

Curtis freed the Moami and held it out to Navaya. She took it and replaced it around her own neck. As it left his hand, he felt a final rush of energy pass through him, as if The Moami was saying goodbye.

A huge wave surged toward them and he ducked again. Beneath the surface a black shadow rocketed upwards, ambushing him from below in the style of a Great White Shark hunting its prey. The Glynt struck his board at full force, knocking him from it. It was only when he found himself in free-fall that he realised it must have bitten through his leg rope.

Untethered, his world turned upside down and inside out. He whipped his head from side to side in anticipation of another attack, but the churning water offered zero visibility. In the surprise of the ambush he'd expelled the breath he'd taken for the dive. The pressure on his chest increased from lack of oxygen, and he tried not to panic against the growing sense of disorientation. The heavy blanket of storm clouds meant there was insufficient light to indicate which way the surface was. He didn't know which way was up, which direction to swim.

All about him the water rocked with the shadowy images of battle, and he knew Glynts and Arax were locked in bitter combat. His fading consciousness dimly registered a writhing mass of bodies, the gleam of emerald eyes, the white points of teeth, blooms of violet blood, and infusing all the putrid stench of Glynts and death. The last thing he sensed before everything faded to black was a pair of Glynts, one on either side of him. With a sudden charge, they came at him, jaws gaping.

CHAPTER 17

He was five again, sitting in a bath of scented bubbles. Mum was washing his hair, pouring clean water from a jug over his head to cleanse the shampoo from his hair. The water felt warm and comforting as it cascaded down across his hair, his face. His mother smoothed the hair from his forehead and ran her fingers through the tangles.

Then she was seizing clumps of it, pulling and yanking. *Ow, mum. Stop it. It hurts.* His head was twisted and pulled through the bubbles and foam until…

…it was Navaya. She was cradling him in her arms as if he really were still five years old. Bubbles swirled past him, miniature pockets of precious air, and he knew he was still under water. He wanted to close his eyes and escape back into the perfumed bubbles of his dream. Navaya had plunged her webbed fingers into his hair, and was using a fistful to jerk his head back. He struggled as she pressed something hard and foreign into his mouth. With her other hand she rubbed hard at his throat until he swallowed. He felt a cold sphere slide down his throat. The urge to gag caused him to open his mouth and too late he realised he'd taken in great mouthfuls of ocean. Salt water hit the pit of his stomach and he knew that unless Navaya was able to get him up to the surface quickly, it would be the end.

But Navaya didn't move. She held his hands and let him become one with the undercurrent. He laced his fingers into hers as his body floated and drifted. He breathed deeply, eyes darting about for any sign of Glynts.

He breathed deeply.

He blinked at Navaya, and then breathed again. He watched in fascination as the stream of bubbles he exhaled blended with others in the ocean. Navaya smiled, then pulled something from a little pouch attached to her tunic. She opened her palm and held it in front of his face. In it lay a small green pearl, round and perfect. It was the same shade as her eyes.

"Araxie pearl," she said. He could hear her under water as clearly as he could on land, but her voice sounded richer, more natural. "It gives the same ability to you that it gives to Glynts on land, but in reverse."

Curtis thought about what she was saying. If the pearl allowed a Glynt to breathe and walk on land for a limited time, then did the reverse mean that if he swallowed the pearl he could breathe underwater? He braced himself and inhaled deeply. The fire had left his lungs and the pressure was gone from his chest and head. He breathed again, marvelling at the sensation. Navaya was right. He could breathe underwater.

"But, how did you know?" he said. A stream of bubbles drifted from his mouth.

"I didn't know for sure." Navaya's shoulders lifted in a small shrug. "It was a guess. I trusted in the lore of the ocean. You've proved yourself worthy of your gift, Curtis." Navaya held out the pearl to Curtis. "Here, keep this safe. It is Araxie's gift to you. You won't need it to return to shore. The Glynts are gone—for now. You may not ever need it. But if a time comes, son of Robert and Lori, when you need our help whether it is now, or in a thousand moon cycles, know that you have the means to find us again."

And from all around him came the voice of the Arax united in their single melodic note. They darted through the water around him, shifting in and out of the shadows. They reached out their hands to touch him as they passed, turning the water into a kaleidoscope of delicate multi-coloured fins.

Curtis closed his fist around the pearl. "Thank you, Navaya.

Thank you, all." He zipped it safely into the little concealed pocket on the leg of his wetsuit.

The sensation of swimming under water was one he would love to have experienced under different circumstances, but he was exhausted. Even though the Glynts were gone there was still the surf to tackle on the return to shore. There was no way he could swim for the rocky shelf beneath The Bluff—the crashing waves would pulverise his body against the rocks. He would have to go back the way he'd come. But where was his board? He'd lost it when the Glynts charged him.

"Your surfboard is safe," Navaya said, as if reading his mind. "Come, this way is up." With a dolphin kick of her legs, she minnowed through the water. Curtis saw a deep gash down the side of Navaya's leg. Several other Arax swimming alongside had also sustained ugly wounds to various parts of their bodies. Curtis noticed one had lost part of her coral helmet. He was surprised to see a sprouting of what looked like coppery hair underneath. He thought briefly of Morgan.

Up and up they swam until finally his head broke the surface. Curtis' first instinct was to gulp in air, but he found that he didn't need to. Above sea the storm had moved westward, cruising slowly towards the hinterland. It was still raining, although a small patch of blue was struggling for elbowroom amid the swollen clouds. The surf was still pounding though, and he knew it was going to take every bit of skill and a whole lot of luck to make it back without getting pulverised.

An aged Arax held his board steady. His face was encrusted with ancient barnacles faded to the colour of old bone. It was hard to tell where his helmet began and ended. Behind it, though, his eyes shone as brilliantly as Navaya's. He touched a withered hand to his forehead in a sign of respect as he pushed the board towards Curtis.

Curtis pulled himself onto his board grateful for its buoyancy. There was nothing he could do about the damaged leg rope however, and he felt vulnerable with the thruster no longer attached to him.

"Goodbye, Curtis," Navaya said. She too touched her hand

to her forehead. "May the ocean's spirit bless your journey home. We were well met. Keep your pearl safe. I would stay with you, but we must return to Araxie before the Glynts regroup."

"Goodbye, Navaya," Curtis said.

And then she was gone. He looked around, searching for the other Arax. The ocean was empty. He was all alone.

CHAPTER 18

Crash. A huge wave almost caught him off guard, but he dived just in time and the mountain of water moved over him. It was time to go. He swung the nose of the board towards shore, and worked on reading the incoming waves as he paddled back parallel to the coastline. Over and under, rise and fall. He didn't feel he'd be in a position to catch a wave until he'd cleared the headland. Onwards he paddled with arms of lead and then finally he'd cleared the headland, and the waves were coming in line-ups he recognised, albeit on a monstrous scale.

The beach looked so very far away, but if he could catch one, maybe two decent waves, he knew the distance would be manageable. He glanced over his shoulder, a monster was building. It gained momentum and height, blocking the horizon. Curtis had never attempted a wave of such magnitude, but if he timed it right he reckoned he could get into position near its peak.

He pointed his board towards land and paddled as hard as he could until he felt the giant wave pick him up. He dropped down the face. It felt like he was falling from a ten-storey building. Curtis gripped the rails and tried to wrestle the nose away from the break. The ocean crashed and thundered. Water surrounded him, and then he was pushing himself up, standing, gunning the board to the left. He powered down the face of the wave and then, miraculously, he was inside the tube. A thrill of nostalgia ripped through him as he sped through the barrel at full throttle. The board became an extension of his body and the ecstasy of surfing charged back into his veins. He let out a roar of triumph and exhilaration. The ocean roared with him.

But then a towering wall of whitewash caught up with him and he wiped out. He had just enough presence of mind to jump clear from his board before curling into a foetal position. The whitewash seized him in its turbulent embrace and he readied himself for the body-slamming destruction he knew would follow. He tried to relax his muscles as much as possible, dimly thankful his board wasn't attached to him.

Curtis tossed and tumbled like a tea towel in a spin dryer. He commanded himself to remain calm and ordered the panic rat that clawed his stomach to be still. But the constant scraping of his body against the sea floor, the helplessness at being at the mercy of the ocean's force overwhelmed him, and he started to lose his remaining composure. It was like when he'd been underwater not knowing which way was up, but this time there was no Navaya to bail him out. His face scraped against sand again and again as he somersaulted like a tumbleweed. He clamped his eyes tightly shut against the churning water to protect against the debris whipped up from the sea floor. His lungs were on fire, the effect of the pearl Navaya had pushed down his throat had worn off and soon the last of his breath would be gone. He tried to bring a hand down to free the remaining pearl in his wetsuit. If he could just reach it—but the water that held him was too powerful and he brought his hands back up to protect his head and face. This is it. *This is it, I'm drowning.* He thought of Mum and Dylan. He thought of Navaya, and Kiara and Morgan, but their faces were distant and distorted. He thought of Dad. *Dad. I'll see you soon. I'll see you—*

And then strong hands were under his armpits, lugging and lifting him from the whitewater. He allowed himself to be pulled through the surf, as limp as a wet tea bag, until he felt the hard surface of the beach beneath him. His rescuer gently laid him on the sand and leant over him.

"Curtis. Curtis. Look at me. You okay, bro?" Dylan snapped his fingers in front of Curtis' eyes. Curtis blinked, focused and looked up at him.

"Dylan? But..." He was overcome by a bout of coughing. He sat up hacking and retching, spitting up gluts of salt water that came from somewhere deep in his gut. Dylan thumped his back.

"I don't know what possessed you to go out there. You're crazier than a snake, Curtis. But I have to say, that was totally epic. You were rad out there. Even if you did wipe out."

Curtis could only nod weakly. He could tell by the way Dylan was gabbling, his words tumbling over the top of each other, that his brother was as shaken up as he felt. He was just trying to play it cool.

"What the hell were you doing out there anyway? Some kind of suicide mission?" Dylan looked at the surf, shaking his head. "You were lucky in a way that you did get thrashed. The white wash bought you close enough to shore for me to reach you."

Curtis nodded again. He couldn't think of anything to say.

"Well?"

"What?"

"What made you go out there?" Dylan repeated. "You don't pick up a board for months, and all of a sudden you're Laird Hamilton?"

"I just had to," Curtis said. It was as true as anything else.

To Curtis' surprise, Dylan didn't push the issue. "I'm just glad you're okay, bro. I thought I'd lost you for a moment there. When you bailed with Dad's board I followed you down to the beach. I knew I couldn't let you go out there. But there was no sign of you until you popped up on that monster wave. Do you know how that made me feel? Knowing you were out there, but not being able to see you?" Dylan's chin trembled. He cleared his throat and jumped up quickly. The thruster had washed up a short distance down the beach and Dylan jogged to retrieve it.

Curtis pulled his knees up to his chest and shivered. The

rain had slowed to a misty drizzle. He felt like he'd been put into a sack and beaten, his body grazed and bruised from the pounding it had copped from the ocean's floor.

Dylan stuck the board upright in the sand next to them. "Amazed she didn't snap in half," he said. "What happened to the leg rope?" Dylan inspected the clean break in the leash.

"Dunno," Curtis lied, looking at the remaining length still attached to his ankle. "Must've just snapped, I guess."

"Everything just snaps sometimes," Dylan said quietly. He hunkered down next to Curtis and looked out to sea for a long time. Then he started to talk, slowly at first. "You were so strong, Curtis. Always the strong one. When you choked that day you thought you saw a shark, I hated you. I hated your weakness—didn't want to see it. Somehow it was like the last of me that was holding it together crumbled the day you showed weakness." Dylan blinked and a single tear slid down his cheek. "It wasn't fair of me, Curtis. I know that. Couldn't help it."

Curtis looked at the ground. He couldn't bear to meet Dylan's eyes—they were so full of pain.

"The longer you stayed away from the surf, the angrier it made me. I felt that if only you could overcome it, then I could overcome a little bit of what I felt about Dad's death." Dylan's chest hitched and he let out a strangled sob. "It was *you* that needed *me*. My own little brother and I wasn't there for you."

Dylan was crying openly now. He stood up and brushed wet sand from his dad's board.

"Here. It's yours. I'll never use it again. Never should have in the first place. Dad left it to you. You've got style way beyond your years. Dad knew it, I know it, everyone knows it. Heck, no one could've ridden it the way you did just now. That was beyond epic. It's like you've got a gift or something."

A gift. I do have a gift, Curtis thought, and his hand felt for the little round lump inside his wetsuit pocket.

Dylan held a hand out to Curtis. He took it and let his brother haul him upright into a bear hug. It was awkward at first and then Curtis hugged him back. Dylan squeezed hard.

"Ow," Curtis said. "Watch my ribs."

"Sorry, bro," Dylan said. "Come on, let's go home." He tucked the board under his arm and they headed up the beach together. As they reached the foreshore, Curtis turned back for a final look at the ocean. He knew he'd never be able to think of it the same way. Now it was a world not just of sharks and dolphins, whales and surfing. It also belonged to Arax and Glynts.

"Seeing your girlfriend today?"

"She's not my girlfriend," Curtis said.

"You could do worse. All that red—excuse me, copper hair—and freckles. She's kind of cute. Mum really liked her. Kiara too."

"She's not my girlfriend," Curtis repeated, and swung a weak punch at Dylan's arm.

"Suit yourself." Dylan dodged the punch easily. "She lost Kiara's necklace, you know? She was holding it for her at The Yell, but dropped it when all that craziness went down. We all spent ages looking for it, but it didn't turn up." Dylan gave Curtis a sidelong look.

"Oh," Curtis said. He could feel Dylan's eyes on him. "That's a shame."

"Why do I get the feeling there's a lot more to the story than meets the eye?" Dylan paused, waiting for Curtis to say something. When he didn't, Dylan sighed and continued, "Oh well, suit yourself. One day you'll tell me, maybe. It's got to be at least breakfast time. Let's smash some bacon and eggs. I'm starving."

Curtis realised he was famished too.

"Maybe Mum will whip up some of her pancakes too," Dylan added.

"You didn't tell her anything, did you?" Curtis asked.

"What do you think I am, as insane as you?" Dylan laughed.

The two brothers turned into Jacaranda Street just as the sun's rays burst through the last of the storm clouds.

CHAPTER 19

Curtis Creed stood facing out to sea. *Come back to me.* The ocean sighed. *Come back to me.* The weight of Dad's board felt good under his arm, and he jogged into the ocean towards the oncoming surf.

THE END

Rebecca Fraser is an Australian author, with a solid career of writing with influence across a variety of mediums. To provide her muse with life's essentials she content writes for the corporate world; however her true passion lies in storytelling.

Rebecca's fiction has appeared in numerous Australian and international anthologies, magazines, and journals since 2007. She actively engages in various writing communities and holds a Master of Arts in Creative Writing, and a Certificate of Publishing (Copy Editing & Proofreading).

Rebecca is passionate about sharing her skills and knowledge, and after several years of mentoring beginner writers and helping emerging writers achieve their creative dreams, she developed StoryCraft Creative Writing Workshops for aspiring writers of every age and ability.

Curtis Creed and the Lore of the Ocean is her first novel. It combines her fascination with the ocean with her love for speculative fiction.

For more information about Rebecca, you can visit her website www.writingandmoonlighting.com, or follow her on Twitter and Instagram @becksmuse

Printed in Australia
AUOW01n1034230718
300467AU00005B/5